DANNY ORLIS
AND THE
ACCIDENT THAT SHOOK FAIRVIEW

DANNY ORLIS

AND THE

ACCIDENT THAT SHOOK FAIRVIEW

BERNARD PALMER

Danny Orlis and the Accident That Shook Fairview
© 2024 by Bernard Palmer
All rights reserved. First edition 1968.
Second edition 2024.

Cover image: Adobe Firefly
Character illustrations: John Ball
Editor: Jon D. Fogdall

Aneko Press Youth

www.anekopress.com

Aneko Press, Life Sentence Publishing, and our logos are trademarks of Life Sentence Publishing, Inc.
203 E. Birch Street
P.O. Box 652
Abbotsford, WI 54405

JUVENILE FICTION / Religious / Christian / Action & Adventure
Paperback ISBN: 979-8-88936-048-3
eBook ISBN: 979-8-88936-049-0
10 9 8 7 6 5 4 3 2 1
Available where books are sold

CONTENTS

CHAPTER 1

BACK TO SCHOOL

Fritz McCloud waited with his dad in the doctor's office with growing impatience. In a few minutes he would be going in to see the doctor. The last time he had talked to him he indicated he might let Fritz go back to school after his next visit. That was what he was waiting for. It was about time he got back to school, he reasoned. It had been more than two months since he injured his knee in the football game and several weeks since he was released from the hospital. At last, his name was called and he hobbled into the doctor's office.

"I think it'll be all right for you to go back to school, Fritz," the doctor said at last.

His eyes sparkled. "That's great."

"But you're going to have to stay off that leg as much as possible."

The lights in the boy's eyes died away. "No basketball?" he asked.

The doctor shook his head. "Not for a while, anyway."

"Couldn't I even go out for practice and shoot a few baskets?"

"I don't even want you to touch a basketball until I give the word," the doctor said emphatically. "In fact, I don't even want you to walk to school until your knee's considerably better than it is now."

Fritz glanced over at his dad. "That's not going to be so easy," he said. "Dad goes to work at a different time than I leave for school, and we've only got one car."

Mr. McCloud spoke up. "I've been thinking something like this would be the situation," he said, "and Mother and I have talked it over. How about going downtown with me this afternoon? We'll see if we can find a good used car for you to drive to school."

This was something Fritz hadn't even thought of. It hardly seemed possible.

They left the doctor's office and went down to one of the dealers where they bought a car that was fairly old but in good condition.

"I think it'll give us a lot of good, trouble-free driving," Mr. McCloud ventured.

The high schooler looked the vehicle over critically. "She doesn't look too bad, for a fact," he said, grinning broadly.

"I suppose you're thinking it's almost worth having a bad knee like you've got in order to get a car."

Fritz glanced up. "Oh, I wouldn't say that. The car's swell, but if I had my choice, I'd a lot rather play basketball."

The following morning he went out in the frigid morning air and started the car. He was pulling away from the curb when a basketball-playing friend about his own age came by. Fritz stopped and opened the door.

"Hi, Johnny," he said. "Goin' to school?"

The lanky senior turned slowly, his acne-marred face twisting into a sneer. "Where else would I be goin' this time of day?" he asked.

"Hop in. I'll give you a ride."

Johnny Larson came around the back of the old car and crawled into the front seat beside Fritz. He looked over the car with admiration.

"Some rig. Just get it?"

"Yep. Had to have something to get to school and back. Doc said I can't walk that far on my leg yet."

"Some guys have all the luck."

"At least it'll get me to school and back."

There was a brief silence.

"Wish I could get my 'bucket of bolts' out of the garage," Johnny continued.

Fritz slowed as he approached the intersection to let another car have the right of way.

"I sure hope I don't have any car trouble. She runs all right now, but I suppose a rod or something could go out most any time."

"That's not the kind of trouble that's tyin' me up."

Fritz glanced at him. "What do you mean?"

"It's my old man," Johnny went on bitterly. "He put my car in the garage, locked it and grounded me for three weeks. Imagine that!"

Fritz waited without speaking. After a time, his companion spoke once more.

"All of that just because me and some of the guys went out one night and had a few beers."

"I can't say that I blame him," Fritz said.

Johnny's temper flared. "You wouldn't!" His lips curled bitterly about the words. "At least you do a good job of making people believe you wouldn't."

Fritz spoke calmly. "You've been around me enough to know that I don't drink, Johnny." There was a short pause. "And I think you know why."

"Oh, sure." Mockery marred his face and glinted in his dark eyes. "Sure," he repeated, "you're one of those religious fanatics. I'd forgotten about that."

"I'm not religious, Johnny," Fritz told him. "I'm a Christian."

"What's the difference?"

Johnny meant the remark to be scathing, but Fritz didn't take it that way.

"The difference is that I've confessed my sin and put my trust in Christ to save me." He paused.

"That's where you and me part company."

"The only difference between us is that I've made a personal commitment of my life to Christ and you haven't. I'd like to recommend Him to you, Johnny. He's got the answers to all your problems."

The other boy flinched as though he had been struck, but when he replied his voice was brassy and taunting. "You should've been with us last night. You'd have drowned that religion of yours." A superior little grin tugged one corner of his mouth upward. "We didn't get home till after three o'clock. The guys had to walk me around and pour about ten gallons of coffee into me in order to get me sober enough to go home. I was stoned!"

Fritz tried to witness further to Johnny the rest of the way to school, but his companion continued to boast about the drinking party he'd been on the night before. Fritz glanced quickly at him as he turned into the school parking lot. His companion's eyes were bloodshot, and his face was white and drawn. He was probably telling the truth about drinking the night before.

Fritz knew the story was exaggerated. The guys at school who drank seemed to spend more time boasting about what they'd done than anything else. And they seemed to get some sort of enjoyment out of making everyone think they were in worse shape from drinking than anyone their age had ever been.

Johnny's expression changed slightly. Fear glittered in his eyes in spite of his attempt to hide it. "I've told you a lot of this stuff because I figured I could trust you." His voice was little more than a whisper. "I'm going to trust you not to say anything to anyone about what I've told you."

"So?"

"So, if the story gets out, I won't have to wonder

how it got out. I'll know it came from you." He leaned forward threateningly. "And if you do blab it, I'll be comin' after you. When I get done, you'll wish you hadn't said anything. Understand?"

"You don't have to worry about me telling anyone what you've told me just now, Johnny. I'm not going to talk to anyone about you. But I can tell you now; the story's going to get out."

His companion's cheeks blanched. "What do you mean?"

"Either you or one of the other guys who were in on the party will get to bragging about the amount of drinking you did, and the first thing you know, everybody will be in on it."

His companion got out of the car quickly and, without waiting for him, strode up the school steps. Fritz stared after him until he disappeared inside. Then, still limping badly, he went into the building himself.

For some reason Fritz couldn't get Johnny Larson out of his mind. If ever anyone needed the Lord, it was Johnny. All during the day he saw his friend's sneering face peering at him out of his books or looking over the teacher's shoulder. That night Johnny was at the top of his prayer list.

* * *

Fritz and his parents were surprised on Friday evening when Connie came home from the university for the weekend.

"I thought you'd be cramming for finals now, Connie," Lester said.

"That's what I was planning on," she said, "but Winnie – she's the new girl I've been telling you about, the one who moved here with her parents last August – Winnie was coming home and didn't want to drive alone, so I decided to come with her."

Disapproval was written on her father's face.

"Don't you want me to come home, Daddy?" Her lips curled petulantly.

"You know we always want you to come home whenever you can," he told her, "but it does bother me to have you neglect your studies by coming home the weekend before finals. When I was in college, we didn't do anything but study the last two weeks before exams."

She came over and kissed him on the cheek. "Don't worry, Daddy. I'm going to get my studying done and I'm going to get good grades on my finals, too. You'll see."

"Sure." He grinned crookedly. "I know you will. I guess I'm just like most fathers though. I want to cross all the bridges for my kids and make things as easy for them as possible."

She smiled. "I guess I wouldn't think you really loved me if you didn't fuss at me about studying and things like that. Winnie says her dad does the same thing."

Mr. and Mrs. McCloud were invited out for the evening. They wanted to stay home with Connie, but she insisted that they go.

"After all, I'm going to spend the whole evening going over my French."

"Are you sure you won't mind?"

"Of course, I won't mind. You and Mother go along and have a good time. I want you to."

Connie went to her room to study and was still at it when her parents left an hour or so later. She sighed deeply and turned back to her books as she heard the door close behind them. She had never minded studying in high school. In fact, she had enjoyed her classes. But for some reason, now that she was at the university, studying was a drudgery. After a moment or two she shoved her books aside and went to Fritz' door.

"Hi," she called out, "may I come in?"

"Sure thing."

He closed the book he had been using and pushed back from the desk.

"I'm glad for an excuse to quit studying trig for a little while."

She sat down on a chair near his desk. For a moment there was an awkward silence between them.

"How's the knee?"

"It's coming." His smile faded. "I can't play basketball yet, but aside from that I'm going great."

There was a brief silence. Once or twice Connie opened her mouth as though to speak, but did not. Fritz saw her concern.

"Is something wrong?"

"Not that I know of."

Her brother's eyes narrowed. "I thought maybe there was. Dad's sort of worried about your grades."

"I wish he'd quit fussing at me. I'm doing all right." Irritation edged her voice.

"He was talking with Mr. Blair the other day," Fritz went on. "I understand his daughter Winnie is on probation."

Connie flinched. "I–I'm sorry, Fritz," she said at last. "I told you something that isn't true. I'm on probation too."

"You are?" he echoed. "Do Mom and Dad know about it?"

She shook her head. "I didn't want to get them all shook up over nothing. I talked with my instructors just before we left the campus this afternoon. They all say that I'll be OK if I can do well in my exams. So I'm not worried – really."

CHAPTER 2

COLLEGE CONCLUDES FOR CONNIE

Connie went back to her books. In spite of herself, the vague uneasiness she began to feel as she talked with Fritz continued to grow. She fought against it. Fritz didn't have to act as though it was such a terrible calamity to get low grades. They really didn't mean anything. After all, she only had to get decent marks in her exams and she'd be in good shape. She opened her French book and turned the pages aimlessly. Next semester she would start out right. She wouldn't fool around with the kids quite as much as she had this year. She would study hard from the very first week and wouldn't cut any classes. It wouldn't be nearly as hard to keep her work up as it had been to try to bring it up after she got behind. That was the most important thing she had learned.

She wasn't really worried about being able to get

good grades if she set her mind to it. She'd done well enough in high school. She could do it again.

She was studying hard when the land-line phone rang half an hour later and her younger brother answered it.

"It's for you, Connie," he called.

She had almost forgotten how irritated that shout of his made her until she heard it again. He acted as though she was deaf or something. She didn't know why he couldn't be grown up, just once.

"All right, all right," she retorted. "I'm coming." She shoved her books aside and got to her feet. "I can't imagine who'd be calling me. Nobody knew I was coming home this weekend."

"Hurry it up, Connie!" Fritz called again. "Or do you want me to tell him that you've got another date for tonight?"

She made a face at Fritz and took the phone. "Jim!" She squealed with delight as she recognized the voice on the other end. "How did you know that I was home?"

"I didn't know for sure. I just took a chance on it. Actually, I figured you might be home for the semester break."

"No such luck. We're cramming for finals right now. Our semester ends next week."

"Oh." His voice betrayed his disappointment. "I guess that takes care of that."

"What do you mean?"

"I was hoping to get to see you tonight," he said, "but I suppose you'll be studying."

"Not all evening." She spoke quickly.

Jim was surprised. "Are you sure?"

There was a brief silence.

"Well, if you don't want to see me–," she said.

"You know it isn't that, only I was thinking about your studies. I didn't go anywhere the last ten days before our finals, and I don't think anyone else in our dorm did either."

Connie hesitated. "I do have some studying to do," she admitted, "but I think I could go out for an hour or so."

"Swell. I'll be over in twenty minutes."

Connie flew to her room from the telephone, forgetting her studies. Ten minutes later she had changed clothes and was sitting in the living room waiting breathlessly for Jim Morgan.

Her brother came to the door a moment or two later and stared at her.

"Hey," he exclaimed, "what's going on?"

"Going on?" She laughed. "What makes you think there's something going on?"

"You're the first one I ever saw who gets all dressed up to study French."

"Oh, that." She shrugged indifferently. "Jim's coming over for a little while, that's all."

"But I thought you were going to study tonight."

Her temper flashed. "I'm going to take a little break. Is that all right with you?"

He nodded. "Sure, it's all right with me," he said, "only from the way you were talking I figured–."

Her face flushed scarlet. "You let me worry about my studies, OK?"

"All right, but don't say I didn't warn you."

The doorbell rang and Connie flounced to answer it. She didn't know why Fritz had to be so difficult. He was worse than her dad when it came to trying to boss her around.

* * *

Saturday morning Fritz volunteered to go to the grocery store for his mother. At first, she didn't know whether she needed anything or not.

"I could use some milk, I guess," she said finally. "But I don't have to have it now. I have to go to the store myself this afternoon."

"I'll go get the milk for you right away," he told her, "if that's all right."

"I suppose it will be." She eyed him curiously.

Connie, who was sitting at the breakfast table, looked up. "What makes going to the supermarket so interesting all of a sudden, Fritz?" she asked, her eyes dancing. "Do they have a new check-out girl?"

"It's nothing like that," he countered, grinning. "Johnny Larson started working there as a carry-out boy. I thought maybe buying some milk would give me a good reason to go into the store. I'd like to ask him to go to Sunday school with me tomorrow."

"Johnny Larson?" Connie asked, her pretty face crinkling. "He's sort of wild, isn't he?"

Fritz did not answer her immediately.

"I always thought he ran with a tough bunch."

"He doesn't have a very good reputation," her brother admitted.

There was a moment or two before Connie spoke again. "Do you think you should run around with a boy like that?"

"I'm not running with him," Fritz explained. "I've just picked him up a few times and have given him a ride to school, that's all. I've been trying to talk with him about giving his heart to the Lord Jesus Christ."

"Oh." She toyed with a piece of bacon still on her plate.

Fritz bothered her – the way he talked about witnessing to the kids at school. He was so open and unashamed about it, as though he were telling the guys how well he liked a new watch or the sweater he got for his birthday.

She couldn't witness the way he did. Of course, it was easier at high school than it would be in college, she reasoned. The kids in college were sophisticated. They had to reason everything out for themselves. They didn't take what somebody said without examining it critically.

Nevertheless, Connie was disturbed and vaguely dissatisfied with herself as she went to her studies.

* * *

When Connie got back to the university she took her exams, but not without a certain amount of troubling fear.

"I don't know how I made out," she told Winnie Blair as they sat in the student union after writing the last exam.

"Neither do I, and I'm afraid to find out."

"I've never failed before," Connie said.

"Neither have I."

They tried to dismiss the possibility from their minds, but it was difficult.

Still, Connie was unprepared for the notice when it came. She sat numbly at her desk, staring at the slip of paper she held with trembling fingers. She was no longer crying, but her eyes were red and swollen and dejection masked her sallow face.

It couldn't be true! There was some terrible mistake. There had to be. The university had gotten her confused with somebody else – somebody with a similar name. That was the only thing she could think of.

Connie's fingers relaxed slightly and the paper she was holding fluttered to the floor. Mechanically she stooped to retrieve it.

Winnie Blair had been sprawled on her dormitory bed, shoulders jerking convulsively, ever since they got the mail that morning. Now she sat up, pushed her dark hair back from her face, and scrubbed at the tears in her eyes.

"Do–do you think it's final, Connie?" Her voice was taut.

Connie swallowed the lump in her throat. It sounded as final to her as a death certificate. They didn't even have the courtesy to phrase the dismissal in kindly language. Your grades are down. Boom! Out you go! A refund will be made for the unused room and board and the tuition paid. They didn't sound as though they cared.

It was a full minute before Connie spoke. "Do you think it would do any good to talk to anyone?"

"I suppose not." There was a long, tense silence. "We were already on probation, so I suppose this is the end of it. Are you going to call your parents?"

Connie paused. It wasn't going to be easy for her to tell her dad that she had been dismissed from the university for low grades. He had spent so much money on her education and had been so concerned about her studying. If only she had taken his advice and had studied when she had the chance.

"I–I think maybe it would be better to call them before we go home," she said. "I don't want to have to do it when I–I get there."

The girls went down to the phone booth in the lounge and called their parents.

* * *

Winnie Blair's father paced back and forth in the living room. If only he weren't so new in town, he could talk his problem over with a friend. He felt that he had to talk with someone. For a time, he stood by the fireplace. Two years before he would never have thought of going to the pastor. Then he made his decision to walk with Christ and all of that changed. Pastor Reeves seemed to be the kind of a person he could call. He hesitated for a moment and then went to the phone and dialed the pastor's number.

"Pastor Reeves, this is Henry Blair. My wife and I have a little problem we'd like to talk with you about."

The kindly voice of the minister made Blair more at ease than he had thought he could be.

"Would you like to have me call on you?"

"We can come over to your home, if that would be convenient."

Before he hung up, he made arrangements for them to go over to the parsonage to talk with the pastor. About eight o'clock they knocked on the minister's door.

"I hope you'll forgive us for intruding, but we had a serious problem come up and we felt sure you would be able to help us with it."

"I'll certainly try."

As they went into the living room and were seated, Mrs. Blair began to apologize for intruding.

"I told Henry I didn't want to come over this way and burden you with our problems, but he said he didn't think you would mind."

"Certainly not. In fact, I had hoped to drop by and visit you soon."

"This is quite a personal problem," he continued,

"but our daughter Winifred was dismissed from the university today because of her poor grades."

"Oh, I'm sorry. That's very unfortunate."

Henry Blair's temper bristled. "It's not only unfortunate, it's absolutely uncalled for. She was a good student all during high school; in fact, she could have gotten into almost any of the better schools in the country as far as her grades were concerned. The simple truth is that she was fooling around when she should have been studying."

"Now, Henry," his wife said.

"Well, it's the truth, no matter how you look at it."

She settled back in her chair, and it looked as though she had been crying.

"What is it that you'd like me to do?"

Mr. Blair's expression changed.

"Both Nancy and I wanted Winifred to go to Bible school," he said, "but she insisted on going to the university. Now, this has happened, and we think she might be ready to go to Bible school somewhere."

"I see."

The girl's father cleared his throat. "As I remember, you and your wife both graduated from Cedarton Bible Institute, didn't you?"

Pastor Reeves nodded. "It was quite a few years ago, but that's where we got our training."

"I know this is asking a great deal of you, but do you suppose you would be able to contact the school for us and see if it would be possible for Winnie to get into CBI next semester?"

CHAPTER 3

COMING HOME

It was late that night when Winifred Blair and Connie McCloud got back to Fairview from the university. The car was piled high with their personal belongings.

"Want to unload your things tonight, Connie?" her girl friend asked, making no attempt to hide the misery in her voice.

She shook her head. "If you don't mind, I think I'll wait until morning."

"That's fine with me." She pulled up in front of the McCloud house and stopped.

"Good-night."

Winnie tried to smile. "I hope things don't go too tough for you."

Mr. and Mrs. McCloud were waiting up for Connie. The instant she stepped up on the porch they came to the front door to meet her.

"Hello, Connie." There was a crooked little smile on her dad's face. Connie tried to speak to him, but she wasn't able to. She stopped just inside the front door and set down her overnight case. Tears slipped from her eyelids and trickled down her cheeks. She looked from one to the other, desperately.

"Oh, Mother!" she cried.

With that Connie threw herself into her mother's arms. The next few minutes both of them cried a little. After a time, Mrs. McCloud guided her to the sofa.

"There's no need to cry, Connie," she said quietly. "It's all over now. There isn't anything any of us can do about it."

The girl looked up. "But it's not all over," she protested. "Everybody in town will know that I was expelled from the university, Mother. I–I've never been so humiliated in my whole life. I'll never be able to face anyone again."

"Oh, yes, you will," Mrs. McCloud assured her.

It was a minute or two before Connie could continue. When she did speak once more her words were disjointed and expressionless.

"Winnie's parents wanted her to go to CBI in the first place," Connie said, "but she decided on the university." She lifted her gaze to look across the room at her dad. "We got to talking about it on the way home and were wondering if, maybe God is using this to show us that we should go there to school."

"I'd rather think God is showing you that you should study, wherever you go to school," Mr. McCloud told her.

Her gaze met his. "Daddy! Don't joke! I'm serious. What would you think if I decided to go to CBI this semester?"

"I thought you didn't want to go to Bible school," he said.

"That was before I – before this happened," she said. "Anything would be better than staying here and–and having to make explanations to every person I meet."

For a moment or two Mr. McCloud was silent.

"Well," he said at last, "we can talk about that in the morning. You're tired and upset now."

Connie went to bed then, but not to sleep. Every time she closed her eyes, she could see that dreadful slip of paper that had informed her she was expelled. It still seemed like some awful nightmare.

It wouldn't have been so bad if she could have stayed on in the city. If she could have done that, only a few would have known she was not attending the university the second semester. But as it was, she had to come home. Now everyone would know that she had been asked to leave.

Connie didn't sleep well that night. And as soon as her mother and dad got up the next morning, she did the same. They were both in the kitchen when she came in.

"I didn't expect to see you up so early," her dad said.

"I couldn't sleep." Connie pulled out a chair and sat down.

For a time silence hung, strained and tense, over them.

"Have you thought any more about going to school this semester?" her dad asked.

She nodded.

"I think I'd like to go to CBI, if I can get in."

Her dad's gaze met hers.

"Why?" His question was simple and direct, but it drove to the very depths of her being.

"I–I–," she stammered.

"Going to Bible school because you feel that's the place the Lord wants you to go, Connie, is one thing," he said. "It's something else to be dismissed from another school and decide to go to Bible school so you won't have to stay home and face people." The corners of his mouth tightened. "Besides, I don't think there's a chance for you to get into CBI this semester. Classes have already started, and it would be a couple of weeks more before your application could be processed."

"Couldn't we try?"

"I doubt if it would do any good." He sat down across from her. "No Bible institute or any other school is anxious to pick up the students who have failed at some other school."

She reached over and picked up a spoon, twisting it nervously between her fingers. What her dad said was true, she supposed, but it wasn't going to make it any easier for her. That was sure.

* * *

Pastor Reeves and his wife were having breakfast at about the same time.

"I've been doing a lot of thinking about trying to help the Blair girl get into CBI," he said.

"I knew something was troubling you."

"Well, I don't see how I can do it. It isn't fair to the school to try to influence them to take a girl like that. After all, why would CBI want to take her? She's just been dismissed from the university for doing failing work."

Mrs. Reeves poured some more coffee. "I wondered at the time what you were going to do about it," she said, "but how are you going to tell Mr. Blair? You know he's just a new Christian and he did come to you for help."

"I know that." He spoke carefully. "And I don't want to do anything to hurt him, but at the same time, I can't do anything that might hurt Cedarton Bible Institute either."

Once more the minister's wife sat down across from him. "With a mature Christian there wouldn't be any problem," she went on, "but do you think they're ready to take something like this? Do you think they'll understand?"

Pastor Reeves pulled in a long, deep breath and expelled the air slowly. "We'll have to pray that they will understand," he said.

The pastor had just finished breakfast and was getting ready to go to the church to his study when Henry Blair and his daughter drove up. The tall businessman introduced his daughter to the minister.

Pastor Reeves showed them into the living room and sat down. For a minute or two silence reigned. Mr. Blair squirmed uneasily in his chair. It was some time before he spoke.

"You know, pastor, when my wife and I were here last night we talked with you about helping Winnie get into Cedarton Bible Institute."

The pastor nodded.

"Well," Mr. Blair continued, "she's decided to go."

Winnie broke in quickly. "But not now. I'm going to start next September."

"That's right," her father went on. "We talked it out this morning and thought that would be best. When Winnie called yesterday afternoon, I knew it would be hard for her to come back to Fairview and have to answer all the questions people would ask her. I didn't realize it when we came over here last night, but I see now that I was only trying to protect her at the expense of CBI."

"And we don't want to do that," the girl said. "I know it will be hard for me, but I'm going to stay here in Fairview and get a job until time for school to start next September."

"I'm certainly glad to hear you say that," the minister said. "I was going to call you this morning and tell you that I didn't feel I could ask CBI to take Winnie under these circumstances."

"Well, I want to apologize for trying to use you. As a businessman before I committed my life to Christ,

I always tried to use anything and anyone I could to further my own ends. I've had a hard time getting over that since I've been a Christian."

"I can understand just how it is."

"My wife and I sat up for a long while last night talking about this very thing. We finally decided that the Lord must be trying to teach Winnie and Connie something through this dismissal. If we could get them into another school – which I doubt would be possible under the circumstances and at this late date – we might be interfering with God's plan for their lives."

Pastor Reeves nodded gravely. "This is one decision I'm sure that you will not be sorry about," he said.

Winnie smiled weakly. "It's hard for me to say this because it–it's not going to be easy to face people around town for a while, but I know it's best for me."

Pastor Reeves smiled reassuringly. "I'm sure it is. Mrs. Reeves and I will be praying for you."

When the visitors were finally gone Pastor Reeves turned to his wife. "That's one problem that wasn't difficult to solve," he said. "Blair might not have known Christ very long, but he's got more under-standing than a lot of men who have been Christians for twenty years. He's really learned to put Christ first in his life."

* * *

Fritz thought he should be able to go out for basketball a week or two after he went back to school, but the doctor still refused to give his permission.

"If we aren't careful, we could undo all that's been done."

Concern gleamed in Fritz' eyes. "Think I'll be able to play next week?" he asked.

"Come back and see me in two weeks. We'll talk about it then."

"Is that a promise?"

"It's a promise that we'll talk about it. I want you to remember that I'm not actually promising anything more than that."

Although he was not limping as much as he had been when he first went back to school, Fritz stayed off his leg as much as possible and drove wherever he went. Several mornings a week he made a special effort to find Johnny Larson and give him a ride to school.

"I sure appreciate this, Fritz," Johnny said. "As soon as I get on wheels again, I'll try to make it up to you."

"That's OK."

"No, it isn't. I want to show you how much I appreciate it."

Fritz glanced in his direction. "If you really want to show your appreciation. I've got a swell idea. How about going to Bible Club with me Thursday night?"

Johnny's face clouded. "What?"

"I'd like to have you go to Bible Club with me Thursday night."

"Bible Club?" There was suspicion in Johnny's voice. "What's that?"

"You know about our Bible Club, don't you?" Fritz asked. "We meet over at Danny Orlis' every Thursday night."

Johnny settled back in the seat.

"I'll make you a deal, Fritz," he said. "I'll go to your party on Thursday night if you'll go to my party Saturday night."

Fritz turned into the school parking lot and braked to a stop.

"Are you talking about the kind of party that caused you to get grounded?"

His companion grinned. "Now, what makes you think I'd go to another party like that? I've reformed – or didn't you know?"

The boys got out of the car and started up to the schoolhouse.

"I couldn't make a deal like that with you, Johnny," he said. "I think you know that without my telling you. I don't go to that kind of party."

"Aw, come off it. It's all right to make your parents think you're a little plaster saint, but I don't buy that. I know you want to have fun the same as the rest of us."

"Sure, I want to have fun," Fritz acknowledged. "Only that's not my idea of fun."

His friend laughed. "Well," he said, "I guess I do owe you something. My old man's started treating me as though I'm halfway human since I told him that I've been running around with you. I might be able to con him into letting me have my car back, if he thinks I'm going to be a good boy from now on."

"Then you'll go to club with me?" Fritz urged.

"I'll think that one over and let you know."

But his tone of voice was more friendly and reassuring than any time since Fritz had started hauling him to school.

"I'll see you Thursday after school."

Johnny's grin widened. "I'd go for sure if you'd promise to come to our party," he said. "That's the kind of a guy I am."

Fritz did not answer him.

The next two days he prayed often for Johnny Larson, asking God to open his heart and make him willing to go to Bible Club and listen to the gospel.

"Help me pray for him, will you, Connie?" Fritz asked Connie one evening that week.

She looked up from her dusting. "Of course, I will," she said, "but do you think it will do any good? I mean, he seems so hard and arrogant and overbearing."

"That's just the kind of a guy who needs Christ," Fritz said quietly.

CHAPTER 4

THE EX-STUDENT REBELS

Fritz waited for Johnny Larson in the hall outside his last class Thursday afternoon. One corner of Johnny's mouth lifted into a crooked grin as he saw him.

"Hi," Fritz spoke to him.

"I sure didn't expect to meet you out here this afternoon – or did I?" Johnny replied.

The injured basketballer walked down the corridor with the other boy.

"How's the knee?" Johnny asked, his expression changing.

"It's getting better all the time." Fritz paused. "How about Bible Club tonight? Are you still planning on going with me?"

Johnny stopped. His grin faded and the lights died in his eyes. "I've been doing a lot of thinking about that," he said. "I haven't got any business going to a place where they study the Bible. I don't know a thing about it."

"Then you'll be in good company. None of us do."

"I'd just make a fool of myself."

"No, you wouldn't," Fritz assured him. "You don't have to speak out unless you want to. If you'd rather, you can just sit and listen."

Johnny seriously considered what Fritz said.

"Well, in that case I might try it – once. But just remember, if that Orlis asks me anything I'm gettin' up and walkin' out of there, and I'll never go back! I'm warning you."

Fritz was so excited about Johnny going with him to club that night he could scarcely eat dinner. Half an hour before time for club to start he drove over to the Larson home and went to the door. Johnny's father answered his knock.

"I'm sorry," Mr. Larson said, "but Johnny isn't here. He went out someplace as soon as he finished eating."

"He did?" Disappointment edged Fritz's voice.

"He said if you came for him that we should tell you something came up so he couldn't go with you tonight."

"I see." Fritz turned reluctantly away. This was something he hadn't figured on. He had been so sure Johnny was going to Bible Club with him. There was a numbing ache in the pit of his stomach. "Thanks," he called over his shoulder.

Bible Club was as good as always. In fact, the

discussion was particularly challenging, but Fritz had difficulty in keeping his mind on what was said. All he could think about was Johnny. Danny Orlis noted his concern and asked him to stick around for a while after club was over.

When the other kids were gone Danny turned to him. "I couldn't help noticing that you seem terribly disturbed about something tonight, Fritz," he said. "Is there something wrong?"

The boy shook his head. "Not really," he answered. "I mean, not with me. But I have got a problem. I've been concerned about Johnny Larson."

Briefly he related the story. Danny listened without comment until he finished.

"I know a little about Johnny," he said at last, "and what I know isn't very good. I understand that he's been causing his parents a great deal of heartache."

"When he finally agreed to go to club with me tonight, I was so excited I could hardly wait to go over after him." The hurt began to grow in his eyes. "But when I got there, he had already gone."

"That's too bad, Fritz. Bible Club would have been good for him."

The high school boy nodded. "That's the way I figured. I could see him getting interested in the gospel and maybe changing his life, but I'm awful discouraged now. I don't think we've got a chance of reaching him."

Danny leaned back in the chair and crossed his

legs. "That may be," he said, "but I can tell you this much, Fritz. That's exactly the way Satan wants you to feel. He wants you to get so discouraged over Johnny that you'll give up on him. And that's just what you can't do. You've got to stay in there and fight, whether it looks hopeless or not."

Fritz leaned forward earnestly. "But what can we do to help him, Danny?" he asked. "If he won't listen when we try to talk to him about Christ and he won't come to club or Sunday school or church, what can we do?"

"The most important thing we can do right now is to pray for him, that God will open his heart."

Before Fritz went home that evening, Danny and Kay knelt with him and prayed for Johnny.

* * *

For two weeks or so after Connie and Winnie were dismissed from the university for low grades, they didn't go out much. While it was difficult for both of them, Winnie found it easier than Connie did. She was so new in town that she was acquainted with comparatively few people, while Connie knew everybody. Wherever she went someone stopped her and expressed surprise that she wasn't going to school that semester. Some took her simple statement that she wasn't going that semester and let it drop, but others pressed until she felt compelled to give them the whole story. She tried to act as though it didn't matter to her, but it bothered her a great deal. She called Winnie on the phone and complained about it.

"I'm getting so sick of answering questions about why I'm not in school this semester I could die."

"I know just what you mean," Winnie replied. She felt the same way when somebody questioned her.

"Daddy could have gotten me into CBI if he'd wanted to." Her voice took on an edge of bitterness. "But he wouldn't."

"I don't think either one of us could have gotten into CBI this year, Connie," her friend said. "The second semester had already started when—when we left the university. Besides, neither of us had much of a record to offer. I don't think they would have looked any farther than our grades."

"That's what Daddy told me, and at first, I thought he was right. But then I got to thinking about it." Connie lowered her voice. "Daddy gives money to CBI three or four times a year. If he'd reminded them of that, they'd have found room for you and me. But no! He wouldn't even call the school and see if they'd let me in. He said I'd have to do it myself. And you know what kind of a chance I'd have had if I'd called them."

The trouble was, she told herself as she hung up, her parents were always trying to run her life. They didn't realize she was grown up and knew what she wanted to do. She was still their little girl as far as they were concerned. They wanted to dictate every move she made. They kept talking about wanting to help her, but when they had a chance to do something that would really help, they wouldn't do it. They seemed to enjoy seeing her so miserable.

She stormed out of the living room and into her bedroom where she stared out the window across the bleak snowdrifts. Tears flooded her eyes.

This was all her dad's fault. If he cared anything about her, he'd have called CBI and gotten them to let her go there to school this semester. She and Jim would be together now and the whole horrible mess at the university would be forgotten. She wouldn't be the talk of Fairview.

She threw herself on the bed and sobbed out her disappointment and frustration.

* * *

Sunday morning Fritz got up at the usual time, put on his good suit and sat down to review his Sunday school lesson. He was still studying when Mrs. McCloud came into the living room at eight-thirty.

"Isn't Connie up yet?" she asked.

"I haven't seen her."

"She'll have to hurry or she'll be late for Sunday school." Her mother went to her bedroom door and tapped lightly.

There was no answer.

"Connie?" she called.

Still no sound came from the girl's room.

"Connie!" Her mother raised her voice.

There was a muffled stirring. The sound wasn't intelligible, but it was clear that Connie was waking.

"Connie!"

"Yes?"

"You'd better get up now or you'll be late for Sunday school."

There was a long silence.

"I'm not going," she muttered.

"What's the matter? Don't you feel well?"

"I feel all right." Defiance crept into her voice. "I feel fine. I'm just not going to Sunday school! That's all!"

"Connie!"

"And I'm not going to church either." Connie got up, slipped on her robe, and opened the bedroom door. "I'm tired of jumping when you pull the strings. I'm going to live my own life. And I'm going to start by quitting Sunday school and church!"

Mrs. McCloud went into her daughter's bedroom and closed the door behind her. It was a long while before she came out. When she did, she was wiping the tears from her eyes.

"I can't do a thing with her, Dad," she said. "She just informed me that she's not going to church or Sunday school anymore and nothing we can say or do will change her mind."

She started to cry once more. Her husband put his arm about her shoulders comfortingly.

"I'll talk with her after she's had a little time to

think about it." He breathed deeply. "She's still hurt about getting dismissed from the university. I think she'll be all right when she's had time to get over the humiliation of that blow."

"I wish I could be as sure as you are. She sounds to me as though she's through with the church and anything else that has the mark of a Christian. She told me that she intends to live her own life from here on out and she's not going to let either you or me interfere."

He glanced at his watch. "We're going to have to hurry or we'll be late for Sunday school ourselves," he said.

"But–but what are we going to do?"

He shook his head. "Connie's almost nineteen. What can we do except to pray for her?"

Fritz listened to the conversation without comment. He went to Sunday school and church with his parents as though nothing had happened. However, when they went to the hotel for dinner he didn't go along.

"I think I'll see if Connie wants to go out for a hamburger with me."

"Why don't you bring her to the hotel?" Mrs. McCloud spoke eagerly. "You can eat with us."

"I–I'd sort of like to talk to her alone," he said. "That is, if you don't mind."

His dad nodded. "I think that's a good idea, Fritz." When the boy got home his sister was curled in a chair in the living room reading the Sunday paper. She was still in her housecoat.

"Hi, Connie."

She looked up and smiled faintly, but did not answer him. He sprawled in a chair opposite her.

"How about getting dressed and going out with me for a hamburger?"

Her gaze met his uneasily.

"Where are our parents?" she asked.

"They decided to eat at the hotel dining room this noon. They wanted me to go along, but I thought I'd rather have a hamburger or a pizza."

She hesitated. "I–I'm not hungry."

"Oh, come now. I've never seen you when you couldn't eat – unless you were sick or something."

The corners of her mouth firmed. "Well, take a good look. You're seeing me now." Her irritation showed through. "I just don't happen to feel like eating today," she said, "and especially I don't feel like eating hamburger or pizza."

He shrugged his shoulders: "OK. We can go down to the hotel with Mom and Dad if you want. They said for us to come down."

Her eyes flashed. "Maybe I don't want to be around them," she retorted. "Did you ever think of that?"

Fritz' eyes met hers. "Take it easy, Connie," he said firmly. "They're our parents."

Anger smoked across her attractive young face. "Now you're trying to tell me what to do!" She leaped to her feet. "I've just about had it as far as all of you are concerned!" With that she stomped into her bedroom and slammed the door. Fritz stared after her, bewilderment growing in his eyes.

He had planned on talking with Connie about her relationship with the Lord, and how she had to get right with Him if she was going to be happy. But there was no chance of talking to her now. She wouldn't listen.

CHAPTER 5

BACK WITH BASKETBALL

When Fritz went back to the doctor the following afternoon he had good news for him. "If you'll promise to take it easy, I think I'm going to be able to let you go out for basketball now."

The boy's eyes brightened. "Do you really mean that?"

"Yes," Dr. Walsh told him, "I mean it – that is, if you take it easy."

"That's great!"

The following afternoon Fritz went down to the locker room. The guys crowded about him excitedly.

"You mean your knee's OK?" one of them asked. "You can play now?"

"Doc said I could go out for practice, if I take it easy."

"Having you back is the best news we've had for a long time. We'll really be able to roll now."

Johnny Larson grinned at him and waved from across the floor. Fritz stepped out on the basketball court and took a pass from Johnny. It was good to have a basketball in his hands again. He had almost forgotten the smooth feel of the ball – the way it balanced in his hand. He had almost forgotten what it was like to take a bulletlike pass, fake the man guarding him out of position, and dribble in close for a setup. It was good to be playing basketball again.

It wasn't long until Fritz became aware of the fact that his lack of practice was going to make a big difference in the way he was able to play. The other regulars were smooth and effortless in their ball handling. Their moves were crisp and clean, where he was clumsy. It was apparent to everyone that his lack of practice had hurt him much more than anyone had supposed it would.

The coach called him to one side when the session was over.

"It's good to have you back, Fritz."

"It's good to be practicing again, but I'm mighty rusty. I can tell you that much."

"That's what I want to talk with you about, Fritz. The other guys have got a couple of months' practice on you."

He nodded silently.

"Fritz, I'd like to put you into your old starting position, but that wouldn't be fair to the school or the rest of the team. You simply aren't able to play the caliber of basketball that's being played now."

Fritz swallowed hard. This was something he hadn't anticipated. He had thought that as soon as he was able, he would go out for basketball and assume his former position in the starting five.

"You–you mean you don't want me to come out for basketball anymore?" he asked.

"Oh, no. Not that." The coach spoke quickly. "I think you will get in shape fast. By the end of the season we may be depending on you a great deal. But right now, I'd like to have you play with the reserves. OK?"

Fritz beamed. "I don't care where I play, as long as I get to play."

He gave Johnny a ride home from basketball practice that afternoon. As soon as they got into the car, Johnny turned to face him.

"If I were you," he said, "I'd chuck basketball for this year."

The youthful driver glanced in his direction curiously. "Why?"

"Of all the raw deals this is the worst I've ever heard of. I'd never play on the reserves after I'd earned a starting position last year. It wasn't your fault that you got hurt. They should give you your old position back right away."

Fritz shook his head. "I'll get my old position back – when I've earned it. I don't deserve to have it before then."

"But to play with the reserves after you've been a first stringer. They'd never pull that on me and get away with it. If they tried, I'd be long gone."

"I'm just so glad to get to play again that I don't care where they put me."

Admiration gleamed in Johnny's eyes. "You really mean that, don't you?"

"Sure I mean it. What makes you think I wouldn't?"

"I don't know." The other boy shrugged. "I was just thinking. You are different than most guys."

* * *

Connie and Winnie made the rounds of the business places and applied for work. Surprisingly, they both got on at the telephone company.

"Imagine, Connie, we're both going to work at the same place," Winnie said. She was so excited her thin voice broke. "How about that?"

"I didn't even dare to hope that they'd be able to use both of us." There was a short silence. "Maybe it's not going to be so bad staying home this semester after all."

"I was thinking the same thing. We'll be earning our own money and can get the clothes we want and everything. We should have a ball."

Connie's eyes darkened and there was an ominous tone in her voice. "This should prove to my dad that I'm not quite as bad as he thinks I am."

After a short training period Connie was put on long distance and Winnie on information. The first week of actual work they were both put on the same shift. They had to work late Saturday night. Wearily they left the telephone building when the week's work was finished.

"I'm sure glad this week is over," Connie said. "I didn't know one week could be so long."

Winnie nodded. "I've thought the same thing more than once."

Connie sighed her relief. "And tomorrow morning we can sleep in. Won't that be great?"

Her friend eyed her curiously. "Aren't you going to church?"

Connie laughed indifferently. "Didn't I tell you? I've sworn off church."

"You can't mean that."

The laughter in Connie's eyes died away. "I'm not going to church again until I get good and ready. Ever since I was a little girl my parents have ordered me around and I've had to take it. But I've had it, Winnie! I already served notice on them. From now on I'm going to do what Connie McCloud wants to do, and only when Connie McCloud wants to do it."

Winnie's eyes widened. "Well, I'm not going to quit church, that's for sure. I'd be lost without it."

"Well, I won't." Her voice snapped.

Connie thought her parents would probably have Fritz and the pastor and Danny and Kay Orlis all praying for her and trying to talk with her about the mess she was making of her life, but she didn't care.

For once she was going to live her own life without any interference from anyone!

When Connie arrived home Fritz was in his room. The light was on and the door was open. He was kneeling beside the bed. Her young face flushed and her heart beat faster. Quickly she turned away.

She went into her own bedroom and closed the door behind her. Her Bible was on the dresser where it had lain, unopened, for several weeks. Mechanically she picked it up. It was probably the first time she had touched it deliberately since she got home from the university.

Jim Morgan was probably doing the same as Fritz before he went to bed that night. But then, he was at CBI. She'd probably be doing the same, if her dad had thought enough of her to help her get into Bible school this semester.

Slowly she got ready for bed. With a start she realized that she hadn't written to Jim all week. She reached for a pen and her stationery, but checked herself. She'd have plenty of time to write to him tomorrow since she wasn't going to church.

* * *

Fritz continued to go out for basketball practice in spite of the fact that he was still on the reserves. His eye for the basket was as unimpaired as ever, but with his bad knee he wasn't able to move around fast enough to play with the varsity. In fact, he didn't even make the reserves' starting five. He was sitting on the bench the first half of the Riverton game.

Riverton scored first with a quick drive down the floor and stole the ball from Fairview moments later to sink a lucky shot from out-court. That seemed to shake the Fairview second string. They tried three or four shots in rapid succession only to lose the ball and have Riverton score again.

Early in the second quarter Fairview rallied briefly to make the score sixteen to five. Then the center fouled, and they came apart again. Before the second quarter was over Riverton had rolled up an impressive twenty-three-to-nine lead.

At half time the coach followed the team into the locker room and closed the door behind him. For a minute they eyed him uneasily.

He looked from one of his starting five to the next. "I don't think you could whip the seventh grade the way you're playing tonight," he began, going on to outline what was wrong with the play of each individual.

The third quarter started out as a repetition of the previous half. Riverton stole the ball and drove down for a basket. One of the forwards fouled the Riverton marksman as he shot. The basket counted and he sank one of his two free throws to make the score twenty-six to nine.

The coach turned to Fritz. "How's the knee?"

"OK." He waited breathlessly.

"Good. Go in for Jones."

Fritz peeled out of his sweat suit and limped out to his position. When play was resumed one of the guards fouled the Riverton man he was guarding. Fritz went over to him.

"That isn't necessary. We don't have to play that way."

Dick Harper started to reply hotly, but stopped, turned, and took his position at the circle. Riverton missed the free throw and Fairview took the ball off the boards. Al Tadlock took the pass, dribbled across the court and back again, dodging a Riverton forward who came charging in.

The referee's whistle shrilled, and his hands went up. "Traveling!"

Al cursed under his breath and slammed the ball at the Riverton man who was waiting to take it outside. It escaped his grasp and sailed into the bleachers. Fritz ran over to where Tadlock was standing.

"Watch it, Al!" His voice was stern. "We can't win ball games by losing our tempers. Let's get with it and quit making such stupid mistakes."

The center glared at him but did not reply.

Calmly and efficiently, Fritz took charge of the shaken reserves. "Take it easy," he said. "Don't let 'em rattle you. That's it. That's better."

Under his command on the floor the players quit fumbling and making mistakes. They began to control the ball and to function as a team, using the plays they had been practicing all week. Almost immediately the situation was reversed. Fairview began to score and Riverton could do nothing right; they traveled and threw the ball away and fouled wildly in their attempts to keep Fairview from scoring.

By the end of the third quarter a determined Fairview

five had shaved away half of Riverton's seventeen-point lead to make the score twenty-eight to twenty. At the quarter, the coach talked to them again.

"Now you're playing basketball," he said. "We're going to win this game yet."

Fritz nodded grimly. Losing was hard for him. It always had been – whether it was a basketball game or a game of checkers with Connie. The coach glanced in his direction.

"How's the knee, Fritz?"

"OK." He spoke quickly – a little too quickly. "I mean, it's going to be all right when it gets loosened up. It hardly hurts at all."

Fairview made two baskets in quick succession to cut the Riverton lead by half. The opposing team dropped in a free throw, but Fairview scored again. And when the final gun sounded, they had eked out a five-point victory.

A cheer went up from the crowd.

But Fritz scarcely heard it as he limped into the dressing room. He was standing inside the door, gingerly flexing his knee when the coach entered.

"What's the matter, Fritz?" he asked. "Is your knee giving you some trouble?"

The boy nodded. "A little."

The coach knelt to look at it. It was swollen half again its normal size!

CHAPTER 6

REAPING BAD SEED

The coach examined Fritz' swollen knee carefully.

"I actually don't believe you hurt it by playing tonight, Fritz, but I'm going to have the doctor look at it to be sure."

Fritz grimaced. "Can't we wait and see how it is tomorrow before we call the doctor?"

Their gazes met.

"Now, what've you got against Doc?" he asked. "I always thought he was OK." There was a bantering tone in his voice.

"I don't have anything against him, except that he's always telling me I'd better wait a couple of weeks before I play basketball."

"I know just how you feel. I used to have a knee like yours when I was in high school. I thought the doctor was taking his spite out on me because he wouldn't let me play for quite a while. But seriously,

Fritz, all he wants to do is to see to it that you don't wind up with a permanent injury, if he can."

Fritz nodded. "I guess I know that, but it sure is hard to sit on the sidelines when the team needs me."

By the time he showered and got into his street clothes the coach was back, smiling broadly.

"Well, you get a reprieve," he said. "The doctor said it isn't unusual for a knee like yours to swell after you've used it strenuously. You won't have to go down to see him unless it gets to bothering you."

Fritz sighed his relief.

He planned on getting Johnny Larson to go out for a sandwich that night after the varsity game, but Johnny turned him down.

"Sorry," he said, "but I've got things to do."

"I'd sure like to have you come with me." He had an idea what Johnny had planned.

"We'd be glad to have you come along with us, Fritz," Johnny answered, winking, "if you get what I mean."

"No thanks."

"The trouble with you is that you don't know what you're missing."

It was not until Monday morning on the way to school that he saw his friend again. He stopped beside Johnny and touched the horn. The lanky basketball player sauntered over to the car.

"Well, now, this is nice of you to come along and give a poor 'hung-over' basketball player a ride."

Fritz did not comment.

"You should've been with us Friday night." Johnny grinned crookedly. "You should've been along to help take care of me. Did I ever 'hang one' on!"

"If the coach finds out about it, you'll get clobbered, Johnny."

The boy's eyes narrowed. "He's not going to find out, if you don't tell him."

"You'll tell him yourself. You can't play a good game of basketball and still drink or smoke. You know that by this time."

Johnny laughed his derision. "You sound like my old man when you talk that way," he jeered. "Why don't you put it on tape so you can play it back to me whenever you get the urge to preach? That way you can save your breath. How about it?"

* * *

Later in the week Fritz talked with Johnny again about going to Bible Club with him the following Thursday night.

"It might be all right, but I really should spend the time studying. Got to get on the honor roll and all of that rot."

"Club doesn't last long," Fritz said. "You can study when you get home afterward. That's what I do."

"Maybe." He grinned self-consciously. "Won't they fall over when I come walking in? You'd better tell that Orlis character to have the smelling salts handy. He'll need 'em."

"I don't think anybody's going to fall over in a faint,

but we'll be on the lookout for it." There was a brief pause. "I'll stop by for you about seven-thirty. OK?"

Johnny nodded. "I must be out of my mind, but I don't have much to do this week. I'll go with you."

Fritz prayed a long while on Wednesday night that Johnny would actually go to club with him. God answered his prayer. The next evening when he stopped for Johnny, his new friend was ready to go.

"I still don't know why I'm doin' this," he muttered.

"You'll enjoy it, Johnny. And after you go a time or two, you'll be sorry it took you so long to get there."

"Don't figure on me going more than once. That's about all I'll be able to take."

The Bible lesson that night was in the book of Romans. Danny made no changes because Johnny was there, except to take a bit more time explaining the way of salvation. The newcomer leaned forward, listening intently. He seemed genuinely disappointed when the lesson was over for the evening.

Danny followed him to the door. "We're sure glad you came tonight, Johnny," he said.

"So am I." There was a new note of respect in his voice. "I really mean that."

"I hope you'll come back next week."

Johnny paused. "I just might come around again," he replied, "if I don't have anything else to do."

Fritz said nothing to him about the meeting until they were almost home. "I'm sure glad you went with me tonight."

For a brief instant Johnny was more serious than Fritz had ever known him to be. "It was different than I thought it'd be. That's for sure. I can see why a guy would like to go." Then his eyes danced. "Now it's your turn to go to one of our parties with me. You'll find out that's different too."

Fritz said nothing.

"I can tell you this much right now. After you've been with us a couple of times, you'll find out your kind of party is mighty dull."

* * *

When the last of the Bible Club members had gone and the triplets were in bed, Danny turned to Kay.

"Well, Fritz finally got Johnny Larson here for a meeting."

"He seemed interested too."

"That's what I was thinking."

* * *

Fritz played two games with the reserves before being moved back to the varsity. Playing seemed to strengthen his knee. He still limped slightly when he was tired, but it wasn't nearly as pronounced, and it didn't hurt the way it used to when he exerted himself.

The last game of the regular season he finally made the starting lineup with the varsity and sparked the team to victory. When they went to the district tournament, he was easily the standout on the Fairview squad. It wasn't that he was a high scorer, or a giant on defense who held his man scoreless. Instead, it was a more subtle thing. He brought a certain nameless, cohesive quality to the floor with him that seemed to transcend personal ambition and attempts to star. When Fritz was in the lineup the Fairview five were a team.

Even Johnny Larson, who was always playing for the scoreboard and was more concerned about being a high-point man than in seeing Fairview win, took to passing to someone who was in a better position than he was, rather than shoot himself. With Fritz on the floor the other four seemed more calm and professional. They didn't foul or throw the ball away as often, and when the opposition scored, they tightened their own defense without getting upset.

Fairview won the first tournament contest easily; the second game was a bit harder, but they forged ahead early in the second quarter. Although the score was always close, they did not surrender the lead again.

The final game for the district title was different. Fairview slipped behind in the opening minutes of the first quarter, only to come clawing back to take the lead from Elwood before the period was over. That set the pace for the entire game. The lead changed a dozen times as Fairview dropped behind only to come fighting back to gain the lead once more.

It was a rough, bruising contest and the fourth quarter was marred by repeated fouling. Elwood lost three of her starting five on fouls and Fairview lost her right forward and the left guard by the same route. Fritz glanced about the floor. Only three minutes remained and they were behind six points. His teammates were tense and jittery.

"All right, guys, take it easy." He kept up a running line of chatter. The sound of Fritz' calm voice seemed to relax the other four. When they got the ball, they were as much at ease as in a practice game, moving the ball down the floor with confidence.

Fritz' young voice barked out a command. Instantly the Fairview five put a play into motion with Johnny tipping in a basket for two points to cut the lead to four.

Elwood took the ball outside, but Fritz drove in to intercept the pass and sink another two-pointer.

The referee blew his whistle sharply. "Foul!"

A groan went up from the Elwood stands.

"One and one; the basket counts."

Deliberately Fritz took the ball, bounced it once and shot. The ball swished through without touching the rim. On the next shot he hit the rim and it bounced back. He dove for it just in time to snatch it away from an Elwood defender's outstretched hands, faked a shot and flicked the ball to Johnny who tipped it in.

Moments later the game ended and Fairview was on its way to the state tournament. An excited, laughing basketball squad clowned in the dressing room.

* * *

At school Monday morning Fritz and Johnny were something of celebrities. Everywhere they went kids stopped them to talk about the thrilling finish of the district championship game or the state tournament.

"Everybody's going down to watch you," one of the girls said. "People are saying this is the best basketball team Fairview ever had."

Johnny grinned broadly. "That's understandable," he said. "This is the only basketball team I've starred on."

"If it hadn't been for Fritz, though, you wouldn't have been such a star," one of the boys reminded him. "He fed you the ball to make the last basket."

"Sure, I know that, and I do want to give him a little credit, but don't forget I'm the one who made that basket when the chips were down."

On the way to the gym after school that afternoon, Johnny walked along with Fritz.

"I guess we showed 'em how to play basketball, didn't we?"

"We did all right, but don't forget that we've got a tough game coming up the first day of the state tournament. Did you see who we play?"

"And did you see who are the favorites?" Johnny asked. "We're picked to win by twelve points."

"I wish those sportswriters had to get out there and play in a few of these so-called 'easy' games."

Johnny frowned. "Aw, come off it, Fritz. You know we're the stars. Don't act so modest."

Fritz did not answer him.

In the dressing room the coach got the squad together. Johnny sat down beside Fritz and leaned over to whisper to him.

"You'd think we lost the game instead of winning it."

The coach called the boys to order.

"I've got some bad news," he began, looking from one to the other. "I was visited by a member of the police department a few minutes ago. One of our students was picked up on a drunk charge last night." Johnny's face went white. "Today this boy was questioned and implicated the others, including one member of our basketball team – one of our starting five."

The guys were looking from one to another quizzically. Johnny squirmed.

"Johnny," the coach concluded, "the chief of police wants to see you in the principal's office right away."

The color faded from Johnny's face, and his lips trembled uncertainly. His fists clenched until his knuckles showed white.

"They want to see you right away." The coach's voice was harsh and cold with anger. "I told them I'd send you up as soon as I talked with you."

Numbly Johnny stared at him.

"But before you go, leave your basketball suit."

The boy gasped. "You–you mean you're not going to let me play anymore?"

"Exactly." The coach's voice grew louder. "You've been on my team for two years. You know I don't tolerate drinking."

Johnny's lower lip trembled, and for an instant or two it looked as though he was about to cry. "But–but the state basketball tournament is coming up next week."

"That's right. That's exactly right. You should have thought about that last night."

Johnny looked helplessly at Fritz and, getting to his feet, shuffled out the door. The coach waited until he was gone before turning back to the rest of the squad.

"I wanted you all to be here this afternoon," he began, "so you would understand why Johnny isn't going to the tournament with us. And I thought it might be an object lesson for any of the rest of you who might have the same ideas about breaking training."

For a minute silence gripped the locker room. Then one of the regulars got to his feet.

"You didn't really mean that about not letting Johnny play in the state tournament, did you, coach?" he asked.

"I meant it as much as I've ever meant anything I've ever told you. Johnny Larson has known from the very first day he went out for practice that we do not tolerate drinking or smoking among the guys who represent Fairview in athletic events. When he deliberately disobeyed the rules, he should have known what would happen."

"But we'll get beat without him. We won't last through the first game."

The coach leaned forward, eyes flashing.

"I don't think a player who breaks training means that much to any team," he said, "but I can tell you this much right now. If we can't win without Johnny Larson, then we'll have to get beat. We're not taking him to the tournament with us."

The practice session was dull and listless that afternoon. The coach tried to pump some enthusiasm into the team, but the guys didn't respond. At last he gave up and sent them to the showers.

CHAPTER 7

TO THE STATE TOURNAMENT

Fritz showered, dressed, and went to his car. The ache within him continued to grow. If Johnny Larson had only listened when he tried to talk with him about the Lord. If – he stopped short. Someone was sitting in the front seat of his car. Curiously he moved closer.

"Johnny!"

The boy in the car smiled weakly. "Hi."

Fritz got in beside him and started the engine. His companion moistened his lips nervously with the tip of his tongue and cleared his throat.

"I'm in a jam, Fritz," he blurted. "I'm in a terrible jam!"

"I know."

"That stupid Carl Ames had to get so sick last night that his parents got scared and took him to the hospital. When he sobered up and got to feeling a little better this morning, they started pressing him for information and he spilled the whole ball of wax." Johnny swallowed the lump in his throat. "Now my old man'll skin me alive! And I'm kicked off the basketball team besides."

"This is the sort of thing that happens when we don't let God have control of our lives," Fritz said.

Johnny's lower lip trembled uncertainly. "But we didn't mean any harm by what we did. We just wanted to have a little fun."

Fritz was silent for a moment or two. "There's a Bible verse that has an answer to that, Johnny," he said. "'There is a way which seems right to a man, but its end is the way of death.'"

The other boy's lips curled bitterly. "That's all I need. Someone to preach at me!"

Fritz backed out of the parking lot and drove slowly along the street. "I know how you feel, Johnny," he said at last, "but I can't help it. Christ is the only answer to your problems, just as He is the answer to mine."

There was a long silence.

"You mean, if I became a Christian, God would help me to get out of this terrible mess I'm in and get back on the basketball team?"

Fritz shook his head. "I don't think God would help you get out of the punishment you'll get from breaking training. I think you're going to have to pay the penalty for what you've done. But if you turn your life over to Christ, He'll help you live the way a Christian should and have a lot better time without doing things like you guys did last night."

The interest in Johnny's eyes faded slowly. "My old man's going to clobber me. He'll skin me alive when he finds out." He breathed deeply. "He might not even go to court with me when they have the trial. He–he might just let me go to jail and–and not pay the fine."

Fritz turned up the street where the Larsons lived. "You know, Johnny, if you don't give your heart to Christ, the chances are that you'll keep right on getting into trouble. You'll be in one mess after another."

"No, I won't." Johnny's voice rose fervently. "If I get out of this jam, I'll never drink again."

Fritz slowed as he approached the Larson home and looked over at his companion. What could he say to make Johnny see that he couldn't improve himself without Christ? How could he make him understand that he would keep right on falling back into sin because he couldn't help himself?

The youthful driver stopped in front of the house and his companion opened the car door.

"I'd rather take a beating than go in there and face my old man," he muttered under his breath.

By this time Mr. Larson had come out on the front porch and was glaring at his son.

"Oh–oh," Johnny murmured. "He knows already."

"I'll be praying for you, Johnny."

"Thanks." He swallowed the lump in his throat. "But it'll take more than prayer to get me out of this jam."

"I'm not going to pray that you'll get out of your punishment," Fritz said quickly. "I'm going to pray that you'll confess your sin and commit your life to Christ so things like this won't happen again."

Johnny's eyes flashed. "Thanks, pal! Thanks a lot!" He slammed the car door and strode defiantly up to the porch where his angry father was waiting for him.

Fritz sat motionless in his car for a minute or two. Then, thoughtfully, he pulled away from the curb and drove home. Connie was sitting in the living room when he came in. She looked up.

"Hi."

He only grunted.

"Well," she said, "what's the matter with you? Did somebody steal your best girl?"

Fritz shook his head. "I wish it was something like that." He sat down across from her and told her what had taken place.

"You mean Johnny Larson was kicked off the team for drinking?" Her forehead crinkled. "Does he have an older brother who works for the telephone company?"

He nodded.

"Yeah, Ted Larson is his brother. You remember him, don't you? He was the football player that everybody was talking about a few years ago. Guess he was all-state or something."

"I've seen him around the office since I've been working there." A wistful smile brightened her face. "He's sort of cute."

Fritz stared at her. "What's with you, Connie?" he demanded. "Are you starting to give old Jim the runaround?"

She colored deeply. "Can't I make an innocent little observation without everybody thinking the worst of me?" She jumped to her feet and stomped out of the room.

Fritz stared after her, shaking his head.

His dad came in just then.

"Wasn't Connie in here a minute ago?"

"She was in here all right, but she just left."

"What was the matter with her?"

"You've got me," Fritz said. "All I did was ask about her and Jim and she exploded like a firecracker."

* * *

Connie was working the day shift at the telephone company when she met Ted Larson again. She was sitting in the lunchroom during coffee break when he came in.

"Hi."

She looked up and smiled.

"Hi, Ted."

He looked around. "OK if I sit down here?"

"Certainly. I've got to be getting back to the switchboard."

He pulled out a chair and sat down across from her. He was tall and broad-shouldered and was easily the most handsome boy she had ever seen. He was just the sort of guy a girl dreamed about – dark and curly haired with merry, dancing eyes; and he was just enough older than she was to be interesting.

"You don't have to leave just yet, do you?" Disappointment edged his voice.

She glanced at her watch. "I've got five minutes."

"That's better." He studied her appraisingly. "I sure can't understand why they hired you."

She straightened indignantly. "Am I as bad as all that?"

"Oh, no." He flushed slightly. "I'm sorry. I didn't realize how that must have sounded."

"It wasn't flattery, if that's what you mean."

He lowered his voice. "Maybe it didn't sound like it, but that's what I meant it to be. Look at the people who work here. Except for you and your girlfriend, all the others are so homely they'd stop a clock. But you! You've got class!"

She colored delicately. "Is that lesson one in a course on getting girls to think you're the greatest?" she asked.

"No, I mean it. Honest I do. When I saw you sitting at the switchboard, I just about flipped. I figured there must be something wrong with my eyes." He leaned forward. "But I know now that it's true. You're a real, live person, and you're more beautiful than I thought you were the first time I saw you."

Connie laughed to hide her embarrassment. She had never had a boy talk to her that way before. She couldn't be sure if he meant it or if he was just teasing her.

"Now's a good time to leave."

He looked up at her appealingly. "Do you have to?"

"If I don't, the supervisor will be in wondering what happened to me and then we'll both be in trouble."

He followed her to the door and spoke in a hoarse whisper. "Are you working days all this week?"

She nodded.

"Good. I'll try to be here tomorrow morning at the same time. How about waiting for me so we can have a cup of coffee together?"

"I'll see. But I can't promise anything."

She started to leave, but he stopped her.

"One more thing. Have you got another guy in the furniture somewhere?"

Connie laughed again. "Doesn't every girl?"

"Stop! You're breaking my heart!" He reached out and grasped her arm lightly. "I'm serving notice on you and him right now. I intend to take you away from him, Connie McCloud. You may not know it yet, but you're going to be my girl."

Connie's face was flushed scarlet when she got back to her station. Ted Larson was the most handsome, exciting boy she had met anywhere. Winnie and the other girls would turn green with envy if they knew he was giving her the rush.

Her smile came back. She was thinking that being home from school for a semester wasn't going to be so bad after all.

* * *

The Fairview basketball team went listlessly through the remaining practice sessions before the state tournament. Losing Johnny Larson seemed to take the fire out of the squad. They still handled the ball well, and when they practiced shooting, they seemed to make as many baskets as ever. Only a careful observer would have seen any difference in their play. But there was a difference. A big difference. The coach was concerned about it. The day before they were to leave for the tournament, he called Fritz into his office.

"We've got a bad situation, Fritz. Unless we can get the guys fired up to the place where they believe we can win without Johnny, we're whipped before we ever get started."

Fritz nodded. "I know just what you mean. I've been thinking the same thing."

"For some reason, the more I talk to them about it the more they tense up," the coach continued. "I thought maybe you might be able to help do something with them, Fritz."

The boy scratched his ear with his forefinger. "I don't know whether I can or not," he said, "but I can sure try."

He left the coach's office then and made his way down to the parking lot. Gilbert Owens and Ray Towns were there changing a tire on Ray's old car. They were both on the starting five. Fritz went over to them.

"Need some help?" he asked.

They looked up. "Not half as bad as we're going to need help when we get in that tournament next week," Gilbert said.

Fritz leaned against the car beside Ray's.

"Oh, I don't think things are going to be as bad as all that," he said.

They both straightened.

"Without Johnny to control the boards we're dead," Ray answered, "and it's all the coach's fault. He could let Johnny play if he wanted to."

Fritz spoke quietly. "We're not dead without Johnny unless we go down there thinking we are. We've got a smooth team. Don't let anybody tell you any different."

The boys weren't ready to accept the possibility of victory without the help of Johnny.

"My dad said some of the men around town went out and talked with the coach to see if he would give Johnny another chance," Gilbert said, "but he wouldn't do it." He paused, anger smoking in his eyes. "They even went to the school board and the principal and got it fixed with them. But no, the coach said Johnny had broken the rules and he wasn't going to play in the tournament."

Ray spoke up. "The trouble is that we've got to suffer because the coach won't let Johnny play. I don't think it's fair."

Fritz took a deep breath and moved closer to his teammates. "Listen, guys, the coach didn't make Johnny drink. He did that on his own. He knew it was against the rules and he knew what would happen if he got caught, but he did it, anyway."

Gilbert pulled himself erect. It was a long minute before he spoke. "You know, I'd never thought of it that way before. The coach isn't the one who let us down. It was Johnny Larson."

Ray nodded thoughtfully. "Maybe you're right."

"I know you're right," Fritz said. "All the coach did was to enforce the rules."

"We can't let Johnny ruin everything for us," Gilbert went on. "The way I see it, we've got to go out there and show him and everyone else that we can still win. We can do it in spite of Johnny Larson."

"Now you're talking the way I feel," Fritz put in. "We're not whipped yet and we're not going to be."

Gil looked at his watch.

"I think the coach is still here. I'm going in and see if he'll get the guys together so you can talk to them, Fritz."

A fired-up basketball team went to the tournament from Fairview. Battling desperately all the way, they won their first three games to make it to the class B finals. Their opponent for the state championship was Newell, a scrappy all-senior team that had not lost a game during the regular season. They were heavy favorites to keep their victory string unbroken.

The game started with Newell pulling out in front with a fifteen-to-seven lead at the end of the first quarter. It looked as though they were going to win easily.

But Fairview had something to say about that. They battled back in desperation.

The tall Newell quintet was able to keep them from moving in close to shoot, but Fritz and Gil began popping them in from out-court. Slowly, steadily, they chipped away at the Newell lead. At half time the defending champions were out in front by thirty-one to twenty-five. By midway in the third quarter, however, they had cut the lead to a scant four points and forced Newell to switch to a man-to-man defense in an effort to keep the forwards from trying long shots.

Early in the fourth quarter Fairview took the lead for the first time in the game. They lost it briefly two minutes later, but when they forged ahead again, they were never challenged. When the final gun sounded they were state champions by fifty-eight to forty-nine.

Gil Owens threw his arms about Fritz.

"We won! We won! We're the state champs!"

CHAPTER 8

STATE CHAMPS!

The Monday after the Fairview basketball team won the state championship there were no classes at the high school. The kids reported at the usual time, but at nine-thirty there was an assembly in the auditorium. The school board and half the businessmen of the town were present to honor the team. They called the squad to the platform and after several short speeches, the school board president presented medals to each member.

"We owe a particular debt of gratitude to this year's team for the way they came fighting back," Mr. Eldridge said. "When a problem developed just before the tournament, most of us thought they would fold in the first game. And I'm sure it's no secret that I had a number of phone calls from well-meaning men in the community who wanted us to exert pressure on our coach to suspend the rules against those who broke training just before the state tournament."

Johnny Larson, who was slouching in a seat several rows from the front, flushed scarlet. For a moment it looked as though he might get to his feet and go storming out. But he did not. He only scooted farther down in his seat and kept his eyes averted.

The school board president continued. "Fairview has long had a policy of leaving the operation of athletics in the hands of the coach, so we made no attempt to get the rules relaxed even for a state tournament. Our basketball team showed us the stuff they're made of. They came clawing back to win the championship."

He paused long enough to make the presentation of the medals. Then he went on once more.

"In special session this morning the school board decided to create a special award to be given each year to the senior athlete whose character, ability, and competitive spirit come the closest to making him the ideal of Fairview High. Frankly, this award was promoted by our desire to honor one member of the team who has shown himself to be the sort of athlete any school would be proud of. And, more than that, he represents the finest in character and personality. I'm sure you all know who I'm talking about – Fritz McCloud, I take great pleasure in presenting this special award to you."

The applause was thunderous.

When the assembly was over a number of men crowded around Fritz to shake his hand and congratulate him. As soon as possible, however, he walked away from them and went to his car.

Several blocks from school he caught up with Johnny Larson. He stopped and rolled down his window.

"Hey, Johnny," he called out, "want a ride?"

His friend kept walking as though he hadn't heard him. Fritz lifted his foot from the brake pedal and coasted along beside him.

"Come on, I'll take you where you're going."

At the corner the tall senior turned and fastened his gaze on Fritz.

"What do you want to do?" His voice was harsh. "Rub it in?"

"I'd just like to talk with you for a couple of minutes, that's all."

Johnny slouched over to the car and got in. His misery was stamped indelibly on his face. Fritz glanced in his direction and pulled away from the curb. It was a moment or two before either of them spoke. Finally, Johnny cleared his throat.

"Well, we heard them call you the boy scout this morning," he said bitterly, "and you got your award for being a good little guy. What're you going to do now? Are you trying to earn another medal by making a good boy out of me, too?" There was scorn in his voice.

Fritz paused. Why did Johnny have to be so disagreeable and hard to be nice to? If he did what he wanted to he'd open the car door and let the character get out. A guy couldn't be nice to a guy who wouldn't let him.

"You don't really think that's why I picked you up, do you?"

Johnny's frown deepened. "I don't know what I think." There was a brief silence. "To tell you the truth, I feel like going out and gettin' drunk this afternoon. That's what I feel like doin'."

"That wouldn't help any. It'd only make things worse."

Johnny's voice rose. "Everybody in school knew old man Eldridge was talkin' about me. I'll never be able to go back and face the kids again. I'm ruined, I tell you!"

"I wouldn't say that. It was too bad things worked out the way they did, but it's not the end of everything for you by a long shot."

"It's all right for you to talk. You don't have to face 'em. You don't know how the kids treated me when I came to school this morning. Most of them wouldn't even speak to me. They acted as though I was a traitor or something."

"They'll get over it. In a couple of weeks most of them will even forget that you didn't play in the tournament."

"I'll bet," the other boy retorted. "I'll just bet! I'm branded for life right now. And the thing that makes me so mad is that I'm not the only one who was drinking. I was just the guy who happened to get caught. So I'm the loser and everybody else turned out to be great heroes."

Fritz did not answer him immediately. He stopped at a stop sign and turned up the street where Danny and Kay and the triplets lived.

"That's the way people are," he said. "Getting caught

seems to be worse than the sin. But God isn't like that. Whether a guy gets caught or not doesn't make any differ-ence in God's sight. He knows everything we do. He even knows everything we want to do, or are tempted to do."

His companion stared curiously at him but said nothing.

"In God's sight the worst sin isn't drinking or lying or stealing, although those things are bad enough. The worst sin is turning your back on Him and not accepting Christ as your Savior."

Johnny thought about that for a moment or two. "What do you mean?" he asked thoughtfully.

Fritz told him how sin entered the world, how God gave man laws to live by, but that man couldn't keep those laws.

"The Bible says that we all have sinned and come short of the glory of God; that none of us is righteous. That means you, me, Mr. Eldridge, and every person who ever lived."

The corners of Johnny's mouth tightened and sweat came out on his forehead. He moistened his lips but did not speak. At last Fritz went on.

"But God loved us so much He sent His Son to die on the cross for us, so we could believe in Him and have eternal life."

His companion sighed deeply. "You make it sound good," he said, "for a fact."

"It's the only way to live, Johnny. Why don't you try Him?"

There was a long hesitation, but when Johnny spoke there was a wistfulness in his voice. "I don't think I could ever live up to it," he said.

"I know you couldn't. Neither could I, or anybody else, if we had to depend on our own strength. But God knows that. And He doesn't make us depend on ourselves to overcome these weaknesses and the desire to sin. He promises to help us live the way we should. All we have to do is to confess our sin and put our trust in Him."

For a minute or more Johnny seemed to waver, as though he was about to do as Fritz asked him. Then his back stiffened and his eyes grew hard and cold.

"I'll think about it sometime!" he snapped.

"But–"

"I told you that I'd think about it, didn't I?" Anger smoked in his eyes. "For cryin' out loud, lay off, will ya? I've just about had it today without listening to you preach at me!"

Sorrowfully Fritz made a turn at the next intersection and drove back to town. Johnny had been so close – so very close to making his decision for Christ.

* * *

Danny had quite a lot of flying to do, but Doug and Del were able to take over the work around the house while he was gone. DeeDee helped Kay in the kitchen.

"Do you think Danny will be home tomorrow night, Kay?" she asked.

"That's when he said he was coming."

The girl finished drying the dishes and hung the towel on a rack near the warm air register.

"Was he going to see Jim on this trip?" she asked.

Kay nodded. "He had to stop at Cedarton for a while this afternoon," she replied, "so I'm sure he'll see Jim before he leaves the school."

DeeDee sat down at the table. "Do you think he'll tell Jim?"

Kay stared quizzically at her. "Tell him what?"

"About Connie."

Kay still did not understand. "What about Connie?"

DeeDee's thoughtful young face wrinkled distastefully. "You know, about Connie and that–that Ted Larson or whatever his name is. She's going out with him all the time now."

Kay was surprised, but did her best to keep DeeDee from knowing it.

"Well, Jim and Connie aren't engaged so she would have a right to go with someone else if she wanted to. Jim might be dating too."

But DeeDee didn't think so.

"Not Jim. He wouldn't do a thing like that. And I didn't think Connie would either. She's supposed to be going with Jim. She shouldn't be dating anyone else – especially someone like Ted Larson."

Kay did not reply. She didn't know this Ted Larson, so she didn't know whether DeeDee was prejudiced or not. She changed the subject as quickly as possible.

* * *

The school bus had stopped at a stop sign in front of the telephone office when Connie McCloud and Ted Larson got off work that day. Connie noticed that DeeDee had seen them together and the knowledge flustered her. Color crept up into her cheeks and, almost involuntarily, she stopped.

Ted turned to face her. "Hey," he exclaimed, "what's the matter?"

"Nothing."

"You look as though you've seen a ghost or something."

"It's nothing." She shook her head and laughed nervously. "It's nothing at all. If you're going to give me a ride home, come on."

Once in the car, he turned to look at her. "You know what this ride is going to cost you, don't you?" he asked, bantering.

"Maybe I'd better walk."

"Oh, no you don't." He reached across her and held the door closed. "You don't have to do that. All I'm expecting of you is a date for tomorrow night. Let me take you out to dinner at a little place where we can have a good steak and dance and the bill will be paid in full."

Connie hesitated. She had enjoyed the couple of casual dates she had with Ted, she would have to admit. Even though they hadn't done anything except ride around and go to the cafe for something to eat, she had gone home thrilled with having been with someone like Ted. If he hadn't kept talking about going to dances or the theater or places like that, she would probably have kept going with him. It was tempting not to, but she got awfully lonely sitting at home all the time.

Of course he would never take Jim's place; nobody could do that. At the thought of Jim her forehead creased.

Jim was probably having his fun at school, only he wasn't saying anything about it. She knew guys at the university who had dated at school while their hometown girlfriends sat around with nothing to do. She would be foolish to quit going with Ted now when he was so much fun to be with.

He started the car and drove out of the parking lot.

"How about it? Will you go out with me tomorrow night?"

Connie laughed. "Name one good reason why I should."

"That's easy," he said. "You should go with me because I'm the most handsome guy in town."

"And the most conceited."

"You don't really believe that, do you?"

"About you being the most handsome guy in town?" Her voice trilled gaily. "I certainly don't."

"I'm disappointed. All the other girls do."

"That's very interesting. And why don't you go out with one of them if you are so popular with them?"

"Because I want to go out with you. Does that make sense to you, or do you want me to draw you a picture?"

"I think that would be very nice," she said. "Why don't you draw me a picture?"

He frowned. "I never saw a girl like you," he complained. "The harder a guy tries, the harder it is to get anywhere with you. What's it going to take to get you to be my girl, anyway?"

"Did it ever occur to you that I might have another boyfriend?" she asked.

"Jim Morgan?" He laughed depreciatingly. "That stick? You can't be serious, Connie. A sharp gal like you wouldn't waste her time on a square like Jim."

She bristled loyally. "I don't care what you happen to think of Jim. He's a good friend of mine, a very good friend. If you can't talk about him without making fun of him, I'd appreciate it if you didn't say anything about him at all."

"All right." He was properly apologetic. "I'm sorry. Only he–he doesn't seem to be your type."

"Well, he is my type – exactly my type."

Ted pulled up before her house and stopped. "That's only because you and I haven't gone around together very much, Connie. You go out with me a few times and you'll find out that going with a guy like him is mighty dull."

She started to open the car door, but he jumped out, hurried around the car, and opened the door for her. She smiled and thanked him.

"How about it?" he spoke softly. "Want to find out what real excitement on a date with me can be?"

She paused. If only he had wanted to take her to the hotel for dinner, or to a concert or church, instead of a dine-and-dance place.

"I'm sorry, Ted."

The corners of his mouth pulled into a pout. "Why not? Answer me that."

She couldn't tell him the real reason she didn't want to accept his date. She couldn't have him know that she had convictions against going to the kind of place he wanted to take her. If she did, he'd laugh at her the way he laughed at Jim. And she couldn't stand that.

"I wouldn't want to break the hearts of all your many admirers," she told him.

CHAPTER 9

HANDSOMEST BOY IN TOWN

When Connie was on duty it seemed that Ted was always finding an excuse to go in where she was working. He never stayed long, but there was no misunderstanding his purpose. It made her angry at the time, but she couldn't deny that it was pleasing as well.

"Hello, beautiful."

Blushing, Connie pretended not to hear him. He moved closer.

"I said, 'Hello, beautiful.'"

Deliberately she turned toward him, her voice prim and very firm. "Were you talking to me?" she asked.

"You know good and well that I was talking to you, Connie. Who else would I be talking to around here?"

"I didn't hear my name."

"For cryin' out loud!" He swore under his breath.

Her temper flared. "That wasn't necessary," she

retorted, her voice rising. "If you can't talk to me without using profanity, I'll thank you not to talk to me at all."

"I'm sorry," he said, "but you get a guy so exasperated he doesn't know what he's saying half the time. Why don't you have a heart and go out with me once in a while?"

"After the way you talked just now, I'm not sure I'll ever go with you again."

"Give me half a break and I'll never swear again," he told her. "Just exactly why did you quit going with me anyway?"

"If you don't quit this and get back to work we'll both be fired." She turned her back on him.

"Aw–." He stood there uncertainly for a moment before turning and storming away.

In spite of the way the conversation had ended, a smile lit her face as she went back to work. In all the time she had gone with Jim, he hadn't been as exciting as Ted Larson was. One of these times she was going to fool Ted. If he would only stop swearing and asking her to go to the sort of places she didn't want to go to, she just might start going out with him again. She'd never get serious with him, but she did enjoy his company. He could be a lot of fun on a date.

* * *

That night at the supper table Fritz told the family about some special meetings to be held in Foreston, a town twenty-five or thirty miles south of Fairview.

"According to Pastor Reeves," he said, "the evangelist is a real youth worker. I've been talking to a bunch of kids out at school. I think I've almost got them interested enough to go once or twice and see what he's like."

Connie frowned.

"What's the matter?" he asked her.

"I guess you can do whatever you want to do," she said, "but you can't be serious about getting anyone from school to go all the way over to Foreston just for a revival meeting, can you?"

"Sure. Some of the kids go that far or farther to a dance. And none of us think anything of going sixty or seventy miles to a football or basketball game. I think there are quite a few who will be going to the meetings with me."

Mr. McCloud spoke up. "I guess you've got a point at that," he said, "but it does seem a long way to go to revival meetings."

"It isn't so far, Dad. Besides, some of the kids I've been talking with act as though they're real interested. They haven't come through for Christ yet and I can't seem to say the right things to get them to see their need for letting God control their lives. I figure if I can only get them down to some of those meetings there'll be a good chance of winning some of them to Christ."

Lester McCloud nodded. This didn't sound like the Fritz he had raised. There was a seriousness in his manner and a fervor for the Lord that he had never seen before Fritz had gone to Bible camp last summer.

* * *

The next day at work Ted Larson came into the lunchroom at the same time Connie was there.

"Say, this is a surprise."

He sat down across from her. "Now if you just don't get up and run away from me until we get through talking."

"That all depends. Now, don't try to tell me that you didn't know I was here."

"I have to have some excuse to get to talk to you. You won't go out with me anymore."

"With all of your many female admirers, I didn't think you were missing me."

"You know what I think about those other girls. If only you'll go with me, that'll be the end of them. Just try me and see."

"That's just it. I wouldn't feel right in taking you out of circulation and breaking all those hearts."

"You don't care anything at all about whether you break my heart, do you?"

She laughed at him but did not reply.

Ted changed the subject suddenly. "Say, what kind of an oddball is that brother of yours?" he asked.

She stiffened. "What do you mean?"

"Is he some sort of religious kook, or something?"

"He's a Christian, if that's what you mean." Ice crept into her voice. "Why?"

"He's been talking to my kid brother," Ted continued. "The way Johnny acts, Fritz's got him all shook up."

"I see."

"I sure wish somebody'd be able to do something with that guy though. He's about to drive everyone nuts with his drinkin' and runnin' around."

Connie warmed slightly. Ted appreciated the fact that Fritz had been talking to his younger brother. Perhaps this marked a change in Ted's own attitude toward Christian things. Perhaps she would have a chance to witness to him herself.

"Tell that brother of yours to keep up the good work. We're all pulling for him."

Connie's smile was warm and more friendly than it had ever been to him since she decided not to go with him anymore.

"I'm sure he'll be pleased to know that."

Ted's expression changed. "Now, let's talk about something important – like when are you going to change your mind and go out with me?"

"Oh, I might surprise you sometime," she told him.

His eyes brightened. "You mean that?"

For an instant or two she was flustered. "I just might surprise you sometime, that's all."

"When are you going to do that?" he insisted. "Tonight?"

"Oh, I couldn't go tonight."

"Why not?"

"I haven't put my hair up or anything."

"Don't let that bother you. I don't have my hair put up, either. The fact is, it's a mess." He ran his fingers through his long hair.

"I still can't go with you tonight."

"How about tomorrow night then?"

She shook her head.

"The next night. You can go with me then, can't you?"

Connie hesitated. "Well–"

"Good! I'll stop by for you at seven-thirty and we'll go out for dinner. How about that?"

She brushed her hair back from her eyes nervously.

"I really shouldn't."

"That's all right. You can tell me all the reasons why you shouldn't be going with me over dinner."

When she went back to work Connie smiled in spite of herself. Ted was such fun to be with. She was going to look forward to their date with real expectation.

That night, however, she lay awake for an hour or more. She and Jim weren't going steady, that was true. She wasn't violating any promises she had made to him. Besides, she was just going with Ted for a good time. That was all. She was tired of sitting home night after night with nothing to do. Still, a vague uneasiness enveloped her.

* * *

Johnny Larson was in school the balance of the week, but it seemed to Fritz that he was avoiding him. As soon as class was over, he scooted into the hall, managing to keep a group of kids between himself and Fritz. And when school was out for the day, he was nowhere around. He was not with the other kids the way he had been before he was kicked off the basketball team. He was completely alone. Even his old buddies seemed to ignore him.

Fritz wanted to befriend him, but that was impossible when he couldn't find him. Although he looked for him in school and drove around before and after classes, it was not until Saturday that he was able to locate him. Then it was just by chance that he saw the tall senior going into a little hamburger place off Main Street.

Fritz whirled into a parking place and hurried across the street. In the narrow lunchroom, he stopped beside the booth where his friend was sitting alone.

"Hi, Johnny."

He looked up and, without speaking, crushed his cigarette in the ashtray. Acrid gray smoke twisted up from it.

Without waiting to be asked, Fritz slid into the booth across from his friend.

"I've been trying to see you all week," he said.

"Well, are you getting into the game too?" There was a surly twist to his mouth.

"I don't know anything about any game."

"Sure you do. Everybody in school's playing it." Self-pity dulled his brown eyes. "It's called 'Cuss out Johnny Larson.'"

"I'm not going to cuss you out. I just want to talk to you."

Johnny laughed mirthlessly. "Come off it. I know better'n that. You did your share of cussin' me out Monday, telling me what a horrible sinner I am and how I'll go to hell for sure if I don't change my ways."

Fritz ignored the sarcasm in his voice. He talked with Johnny about other things, about the fishing season that would be opening before long, and about going fishing with Danny Orlis.

"Nobody in this town is going to want to go any-where with me," Johnny said. 'Don't you remember who I am? I'm the black sheep of Fairview High."

"It isn't as bad as all that."

When Johnny saw that Fritz wasn't going to jump him about getting kicked off the basketball team, he relaxed a little. At last Fritz was able to get to the purpose of his visit.

"How about going with me to the meetings at Foreston next week?"

Johnny's gaze focused on him. "What kind of meetings?"

"There's a special speaker at the auditorium in Foreston every night next week. I thought maybe you'd like to go with me."

Johnny toyed with his glass thoughtfully. "You don't want to go anywhere with me."

"If I didn't, I wouldn't have asked you."

His companion pulled in a long breath. "I'll have to see how things stack up next week."

Fritz saw him again on Monday, but was unable to get a definite commitment out of him. But he did not give up. He asked him on Tuesday and again on Wednesday.

"I couldn't go tonight. Too much studying to do."

"How about tomorrow night?"

He shook his head. "There's no use in my planning on going anywhere until Saturday night. It's going to take until then to get my theme finished."

Fritz' eyes lit. This was the closest Johnny had come to agreeing to go to Foreston with him. "Then you'll go Saturday night?"

Johnny nodded reluctantly. "Maybe I'll go with you – if something else doesn't come up."

"Good. I'll stop by for you at about seven."

There was a brief silence. "Who else's going?"

"Nobody. Just you and me."

That seemed to make a difference to him. "OK. If you'll be alone, I'll go with you – just this once."

Fritz spent a great deal of time on his knees the next few evenings praying for Johnny.

CHAPTER 10

SATURDAY NIGHT

At last Saturday came. He got cleaned up and dressed before dinner. Connie, too, was getting into her good clothes. Fritz glanced at her.

"Going to Foreston to the meetings tonight, Connie?" he asked.

She shook her head. "I've got a date with one of the guys at the telephone company."

Realization came slowly to Fritz. The smile fled from his face and his eyes narrowed to thin brown slits. "Don't tell me that you've got a date with Ted Larson!" he exclaimed.

"And what's wrong with Ted?" She bristled quickly.

"You shouldn't go with a guy like him, Connie," Fritz continued. "He thinks he's a real ladies' man and–."

There was ice in her voice when she spoke. "Is it such a sin to be popular?"

"He doesn't usually date very nice girls."

"Well, I like that! Now I know what my own brother thinks of me."

"I wasn't talking about you," he countered. "You know that. I was just telling you what he's like. He does an awful lot of bragging about how far he's able to go with the girls he dates. I don't like to have you go with a character like that."

Connie's eyes flashed. "He's always treated me the way a gentleman should treat a girl. I can tell you that much."

Connie was strangely silent as she walked out to the car with Ted half an hour later. Her talk with Fritz was far more disturbing than she would ever have let him know. Ted treated her with respect, that was true. If he hadn't, she wouldn't have gone with him. Yet, she had the nagging suspicion that Fritz was certain of what he was saying. For one thing, he didn't make it a habit to criticize her friends. He must have felt he had good reason, or he wouldn't have said anything.

Ted glanced at her. "Hey," he said, "what's troubling you? You act as though you're carrying all the world on your shoulders."

She forced a thin smile, but did not answer.

"I know what you need to forget your troubles."

"And what's that?" she asked.

"You'll see as soon as we get where we're going to eat."

He drove south of town on the highway.

"Where are we going, Ted?"

"Suppose you just relax and let me do the thinking for both of us."

She wasn't aware of the fact that he was going to a nightclub until he slowed to turn in the drive. Her lithe young body stiffened.

"We'll go in here and get a couple of drinks before dinner," he said. "That'll loosen you up."

"Ted." Her voice was small.

"Yeah?"

"I don't go into places like this."

He glared at her. "For cryin' out loud! What kind of a wet blanket are you, anyway?"

"I don't go into places like this," she repeated, "that's all. If we can't go to the hotel dining room, or someplace where there isn't drinking, please take me home."

"OK, OK." He was angry, although he made some attempt to hide it from her. "We'll go to the hotel. Or maybe you'd like to go down to that church meeting your kid brother's been pesterin' Johnny to go to." His voice was thick with sarcasm. "Or would that be too wild for you?"

She shriveled inside.

* * *

Fritz left the house a few minutes before seven o'clock and drove over to pick up Johnny Larson. Johnny, however, had driven away twenty minutes before he got there. His mother said he asked her to tell Fritz that something came up and he couldn't make it.

Fritz was heavyhearted as he went back to the car.

He had been counting so much on getting Johnny to Foreston to hear the evangelist.

It was so late by the time Fritz left the Larson place that the other kids from church had already left for Foreston. He was tempted to stay home, but finally he drove to Foreston alone, getting there minutes before the service started.

The meeting was the best of the entire week. When the invitation was given several young people went forward. Fritz was thrilled, but it only made his disappointment that much sharper. If only Johnny had come with him.

Outside the church he met Gil Owens and asked him to ride home with him.

"I guess I can," his friend said. "I came down with a whole carload of guys."

They went to a small highway cafe for a sandwich. The service was slow, and it was almost midnight when they finished eating and started home.

"What'd you think of the meeting, Gil?"

"It was OK, I guess," the other boy said.

Fritz leaned forward. "Have you ever seriously considered the claims Christ has on your life?"

Gil frowned. "Can't say that I have. I don't go much for religion. To tell you the truth, I don't even know why I came down here tonight. I had a dozen things to do that I'd have enjoyed a lot better.

They went over the viaduct and into the gentle curve at the bottom. Fritz accelerated to the legal speed limit.

"You know–," he began.

He didn't get to finish what he was saying. A huge black shape loomed out of nowhere. There was a terrifying explosion – and everything was still!

* * *

Mr. and Mrs. McCloud were at home alone on Saturday night. They studied their Sunday school lesson, wrote a couple of letters, and read for a while. It was almost eleven o'clock when Mr. McCloud went out to the kitchen and began to look in the refrigerator. His wife came up beside him.

"Hungry?" she asked.

"I'm not sure."

"I baked a cake this morning."

"You've talked me into it." He poured a couple of glasses of milk and cut two pieces of cake. After a moment or two he looked up. "Do you know the boy Connie's out with tonight?" he asked.

She shook her head. "I understand she met him at the telephone office."

"What's the matter? Is she tired of going with Jim?"

"I don't think so, but it's hard for a girl to keep from dating when the boy is so far away. She wants to have some fun."

He finished his milk and cake and pushed back from the table. "But I don't like the idea of her dating guys we haven't met. We don't even know if he's a Christian."

They were still talking about it when they went to bed.

Lester McCloud roused momentarily when the clock struck midnight, and again when it sounded the hour of one. He stirred, wakened enough to wonder when Fritz and Connie had come in, and drifted off to sleep again.

Moments before 1:30 a.m. the telephone buzzed loudly. He rolled over, jarred by the sudden buzz of his phone. He was only half awake when it sounded again. Sleepily he got up and stumbled over to the dresser to answer it.

"Hello. Who? The hospital?"

At the sound of the word "hospital" Mrs. McCloud scrambled out of bed and ran to him breathlessly.

"Who is it, Lester?" she demanded. "What's wrong?"

He set his phone down slowly and turned toward her. His face was white and moist with perspiration. His hands trembled as he grasped her by the shoulders.

"There's been a car accident, Vivian."

"Connie?"

He shook his head. "Fritz. They want us to come right away."

Hurriedly they dressed and drove to the hospital on the other side of town. Dr. Walsh was in the corridor waiting for them when they arrived.

"How is he, Doctor?" Lester asked.

Dr. Walsh took a deep breath. "These things are never easy, Lester."

He grasped the physician savagely by the arm.

"He's going to be all right, isn't he?" Their eyes met. "Isn't he?"

"I'm terribly sorry. We did all we could."

Lester McCloud's world reeled about him. It wasn't true. It couldn't be! Fritz couldn't be dead. There had to be some other explanation. Fritz was too vibrant – too alive!

Yet, there was no mistaking the horror in the doctor's eyes. It was all too true. His son was dead.

Dead!

At first Lester was too stunned to think of his wife – too conscious of his own loss. Now he focused his attention on her. Her cheeks were a pasty, unnatural gray and her entire being seemed drained of strength. His first fear was that she would collapse. He enveloped her in his arms. For a moment or two their tears mingled unashamedly.

Thinking back on the events at the hospital later, he could not remember their exact sequence. He vaguely remembered helping his wife into a room off the main corridor and questioning the doctor about the accident. He didn't recall when Dr. Walsh explained what happened, or where they were. He wasn't even sure whether it was that night or the next morning, but he could remember every word as though it was etched in the flesh of his heart.

"Like most accidents," Dr. Walsh continued, "this one was so unnecessary, so uncalled for."

"Was Fritz at fault?" The distraught father voiced the question fearfully.

"The police reported the other driver was drunk. And according to the Owens kid who was with Fritz, the drunken driver was on the wrong side of the road without lights."

Mrs. McCloud gasped.

Several minutes later, Mr. McCloud asked the question that was on both of their minds.

"Was the driver of the other car someone we know? Does he live around here?"

Dr. Walsh nodded seriously. "He's the kid who was kicked off the basketball team before the state tournament."

Lester McCloud gasped. "Johnny Larson?"

"That's right. Johnny Larson."

Mrs. McCloud began to cry again, quietly.

"He was so drunk I don't think he even knows that they put him in jail."

After a time, the doctor insisted on driving them home. Mr. McCloud protested that he could drive, but Dr. Walsh wouldn't hear of it.

"I'll drive your car. One of the nurses can come and pick me up."

When they got home, Connie was there waiting for them.

"Where have you been, Mother?" she asked. "I've been so worried I've just been out of my mind."

When her father told her what had happened, she dropped heavily to a chair. Her face went ashen, and she sat ramrod stiff, but she did not cry or speak. Her lips moved soundlessly.

Mr. McCloud related the few details of the accident that he knew. "It was the Larson boy Fritz had been praying for who was driving the other car."

She swallowed hard.

"Johnny Larson?" She had difficulty in speaking the name.

"He's the one," her dad answered. "Dr. Walsh says he's in jail for drunken driving."

Connie's eyes were wide and staring.

CHAPTER 11

FAIRVIEW REMEMBERS

How they got through the next day, Lester McCloud would never know. He remembered taking care of all the details that had to be done. He remembered Pastor Reeves and his wife coming as soon as they heard of Fritz' death and the comfort they brought. He remembered Danny and Kay Orlis and a steady stream of close friends coming to share their grief. He remembered his concern for Connie when he saw her sitting alone, emotionless and unresponding, as though she had lost the capacity to feel.

He remembered the sleeplessness of the following night and how he and his wife got up before dawn and went out to the kitchen. He remembered how they sat, sipping coffee without tasting it and recalling so many things in Fritz' life.

They were still sitting there when somebody knocked on the door and Mr. McCloud went to answer it.

"Gil Owens!" He could not conceal his surprise. "I didn't expect to see you here. I didn't even know you were out of the hospital."

Gil stepped into the kitchen, fumbling uncertainly with the sweater that concealed the cast on his broken arm.

"I got out last night. I wanted to come over and see you then, but Dad wouldn't let me. He said there were too many people over here."

Mrs. McCloud put her arm about his shoulders. "We're so glad you came."

"I–I had to come over and–and tell you something," he said.

"Yes?"

The boy was fumbling for words. "You probably don't know it, but Fritz did a lot of talking to me about giving my life to God. He talked to all the guys."

"That's what we've been hearing," Lester said.

"I used to want to do like he said, but I couldn't because I–I didn't want anything to interfere with my fun. Last night I–I saw how stupid I was. After I got home, I went to my bedroom and–and told God that I wanted the same thing Fritz had."

"That's wonderful," Mr. and Mrs. McCloud echoed.

* * *

Pastor Reeves was finding Fritz' death almost as difficult as the boy's parents were. He had worked closely with Fritz, especially since the boy had dedicated his life to Christ at camp last summer. Somehow he seemed different to him than the average young person in the congregation. He had been more like a son.

The funeral was going to be a large one, the pastor realized, probably larger than any he had ever conducted. And there would surely be many present who had never heard the gospel. The high school principal had called that morning asking about the funeral so they could dismiss those who wanted to attend. From every indication half the senior high school would be there.

What sort of message did a pastor bring under circumstances like that? What should he use as a text? How could he best take advantage of the opportunity that was his? How did he discharge his responsibility before God?

It wasn't that it was difficult to bring comfort to Fritz' parents. There was grief and shock there, to be sure; but they loved the Lord. He could point out God's promises to give them strength and courage, and pray with them.

He dropped to his knees and began to pray. He had just finished and was getting to his feet when his wife knocked on the study door.

"There's someone to see you."

"I'll be out in a little while."

"He says it's urgent."

Sighing, the pastor went into the living room. He was surprised to see a towering boy who had graduated from Fairview High the year before, but he did not permit his surprise to show.

"Hello, Martin," he said.

The gangling young man was twisting his cap nervously with his hands.

"Won't you sit down?" he asked.

Even so simple a request flustered the caller. "I'd rather stand–I mean–I–I–thank you."

His cheeks flushed scarlet as he went over and sat down.

Pastor Reeves sat across from him.

Martin Shields had grown up in the Sunday school, although his parents were not Christians. He had even made a profession of faith at Bible camp when he was twelve, but during his senior year he seemed to think he was too big – too important for the Lord. He quit Young Peoples and Sunday school and church services, except for Easter and Christmas, and he was living in a way that was not becoming a Christian.

"Pastor," he blurted, "I–I've got to talk to you!"

Pastor Reeves sat back in his chair and waited patiently. He had his message for the funeral service that afternoon to finish and a host of details to take care of. Martin Shields could not have known, however, that he had so many demands upon his time that morning. The pastor gave every appearance of being relaxed and unhurried. He had long since learned that being available and easily approachable to those in need was an important part of his ministry.

His visitor squirmed uneasily and struggled for words.

There had been a time early in his ministry when he would have been disturbed by a long period of silence and would have plied Martin with questions. Now, however, he waited, praying silently for this one who seemed so overwrought. As the minutes passed the college student began to relax slightly.

"I don't know for sure why I came here to see you," the boy said at last.

"I'm glad you did. Is there something I can help you with?"

The boy's face was working nervously. "It might seem stupid to you, but I–I wasn't able to sleep at all last night. I've got to ask you a couple of questions."

"Yes."

He swallowed at the lump in his throat.

"Fritz McCloud was working for the Lord twenty-four hours a day. He was always a testimony wherever he went. I've been just the opposite. I've never witnessed to anyone in my whole life, and I've lived more like Johnny Larson than like Fritz. If I–I've done anything it's been to tear down someone's faith or put a stumbling block in his way."

It was a minute or two before he could go on. Pastor Reeves knew that what he said was true. Yet, he did not tell Martin that he agreed with him. It was better to have this information come from his own lips – from his own realization of the way he had been living. At last, the boy spoke again.

"Why didn't God take me?" he blurted. "I've been

a shame and a reproach to His name. Why didn't He take me and leave Fritz to work for Him?"

Now it was the minister's turn to pause. There were easy answers to questions like that – pat phrases that all too many Christians fell back on without actually understanding what they meant. But he knew that this intelligent, seeking young college student wouldn't be satisfied with cliches and platitudes. He had to have something solid, something he could understand and weigh.

"Why don't we go to the Word of God? It has the answers for us."

For the next half hour the pastor opened the Bible to one verse of Scripture after another, reading it slowly to give Martin time to ponder its meaning. He listened with care, asking questions that were not always easy to answer. At long last the light of understanding gleamed in his eyes.

"I think I get it now," he said. "God spared me to give me time to repent and get back on the ball for Him." He took a deep breath. "Fritz was ready to go. I'm not!"

"But you can be, Martin." Pastor Reeves spoke quietly, but with the tone of one who knows what he is talking about. "You can confess your backsliding and come back into fellowship with God."

Together they knelt in the study and the young college student confessed his sin and asked forgiveness.

Minutes later, when he was at the door to leave,

he asked another question. "Pastor, do you suppose this is the reason Fritz was taken? To make me realize that I was a backslider living in sin?"

"We can't say with any assurance why God does or does not do a certain thing," Pastor Reeves answered, "but it is entirely possible."

When Martin was gone the minister went back to his study thoughtfully and opened his Bible.

* * *

That afternoon people began to come to the church almost an hour before the funeral service was to begin. The sanctuary was filled and still they came. Chairs were hurriedly arranged in the basement Sunday school rooms and Pastor Reeves called a local radio repairman to install speakers in the yard. He came at once but was skeptical about the necessity of what he had been asked to do.

"We've never had a funeral in Fairview that was big enough to cause anyone to have to put speakers out in the yard since I can remember," he said, "and I was born and raised here."

"From the looks of the crowd that's here already I'm sure it's going to be necessary," the pastor replied.

The radioman went to work methodically. Before he was finished the minister's judgment had been vindicated. The basement was filled, people were packed in the vestibule, and people were standing on the church steps and in the yard. Almost half of those present were under the age of twenty-one.

The service started the same as the average funeral; the minister read Scripture and led in prayer. A youthful soloist sang. Then the impact of Fritz McCloud's life became apparent. A Christian high school teacher paid tribute to his testimony around the school. As Young People's sponsor, Danny Orlis did the same for the church.

Even the coach had a few words. "There are certain qualities a coach always looks for in those who come out for his teams," he began. "I suppose you could say we set up an ideal and mentally measure the guys on our squads against that ideal. In the twenty-five years I've been coaching I've never had a boy who came closer to that ideal than Fritz McCloud. He was a leader, an excellent team man, and a fierce competitor. He gave the game everything he had, whether he was playing with the reserves, as he had to do in basketball the first of the season when his knee injury was a handicap, or playing in the finals of the state tournament. More important, he was a gentleman, on the field or off – a credit to the school he represented."

Pastor Reeves was still thinking of his conversation with Martin Shields as he got up to speak. "When something like this happens," he began, "we are prone to wonder why. Why did God take one so young? Why did He take Fritz home when he was living a dedicated Christian life and was actively serving Him? But Fritz' death was not an accident. God makes no mistakes. This is part of His divine plan. Instead of asking 'why' we should ask 'what.' What do You have for us now, Lord? What do You want us to do?"

He went on to speak on the first verse of Romans 12: "Therefore I urge you, brethren, by the mercies of God, to present your bodies a living and holy sacrifice, acceptable to God, which is your spiritual service of worship."

At the conclusion of his message, he paused significantly. It was a full minute before he continued. "I've been a pastor almost thirty years. During that time I've conducted many funeral services. Never before have I done what I'm about to do now. But Fritz McCloud's entire life was dedicated to this purpose." He breathed deeply. "If there is anyone here who would like to become a Christian today – if there is anyone here who would like to take Christ into his heart and life the way Fritz did, I'm going to ask that you stand as a public testimony of that decision."

He would have said more, but they began to get to their feet immediately. All over the church young people were standing.

CHAPTER 12

GOD'S PERFECT PLAN

When Danny and Kay Orlis got back home that evening, the triplets were sitting in the living room, more somber than they had been for weeks.

"Well," Danny said, "did you get the trash carried out and the basement cleaned?"

Doug answered him. "I guess so."

"What do you mean, you guess so?" Danny's tone was serious. "Don't you know?"

"Oh, sure." Del crossed the room thoughtfully. "We got them both done."

Danny saw the look on DeeDee's face. "What's the trouble, DeeDee?"

She came over and sat beside him. "We've been talking about Fritz McCloud and–and our parents."

"I see." Instantly Danny was as serious as they were.

"All three of them were doing God's work," she said. "Why would He let them die?"

There was a brief, tense silence. The triplets waited, eyeing Danny curiously.

"I don't think we can answer that question, DeeDee," he said after a time. "Our ways are not God's ways, and His ways are not our ways. But I can repeat what Pastor Reeves said this afternoon. God doesn't make mistakes. He reminded us that Fritz' death was not an accident. It is part of God's plan. We might not be able to see the answer now, but later we might be able to see at least a part of it."

Danny went on to tell them about his younger sister Roxie, how she died suddenly, and some of the things that happened as a result. The triplets seemed to relax as he talked with them.

The entire family was sitting in the living room when there was a knock at the door and Danny went to answer it. An attractive, dark-haired high school girl was standing there.

"Won't you come in?"

She stepped inside. "I'm Sheila Rust." Emotion still tightened her voice. "You're Danny Orlis, aren't you?"

"That's right."

Kay came up, introduced herself and the triplets, and invited her to be seated.

"You're the youth sponsors at church, aren't you?"

Kay's eyes lit. "That's where I've seen you," she said. "You've attended some of our Young People's meetings."

"It's been a long time ago, I'm afraid." She wrung her hands nervously. "I just came from Pastor Reeves and he suggested that I come and talk to you." She paused as though uncertain whether to continue or not. "I'd just as well start at the beginning.

"Fritz McCloud was a classmate of mine. He talked to all of us about his faith in Christ and tried to–to get us to see our need for a Savior."

Danny nodded. "I see."

"That was why I went to Young People's the few times I did. He invited me. I even went to church once, but I couldn't understand what the preacher was talking about. And besides, I didn't want to give up the fun I was having."

"A lot of us are that way," Danny said.

"This afternoon as Pastor Reeves talked I understood for the first time. It seemed as though a tremendous burden was lifted from my shoulders. I felt like running down to the coffin and throwing my arms around Fritz and thanking him for dying so I could understand what it means to be saved. I just had to tell somebody what had happened, so I went over to Pastor Reeves and his wife. I told them I want to start working for the Lord and–and they suggested I come and see you so I can help with Young People's the way Fritz did."

When Sheila was gone DeeDee turned to Danny and Kay. "There's one result of Fritz' death. I'm beginning to see what you were trying to tell us. There was a purpose in it."

* * *

The balance of the week was one of the strangest anyone had ever seen at Fairview High. The Christian kids carried their Bibles to school with them and, on their own initiative, met in the church after classes each afternoon for a time of prayer. Nobody criticized or laughed at them.

The entire school was somber. There was no discipline problem in any of the classes. Neither was there boisterous talking and laughter in the halls. A hush settled over everyone.

There was a hush in the McCloud home as well. Mr. McCloud went back to work two days after the funeral, but Connie couldn't bring herself to go back to the telephone office that week.

"I don't care, Mother," she said, desperation edging her voice. "I can't go back there."

Mrs. McCloud smiled sadly. The hurt was still fresh in her own heart.

"I know exactly how you feel, Connie," she answered. "It wasn't easy for Dad to go back to work this morning either, and it's not easy for me to work around the house. It would be so much easier for us to sit down and feel sorry for ourselves. But life can't stop. We've got to go on."

A strange wildness glittered in Connie's eyes. "But you don't understand, Mother!" she declared. "If I go down to the telephone company I–I'll have to work with Johnny's brother!"

Vivian McCloud sat down at the kitchen table and folded her work-worn hands. They were trembling slightly.

"I can understand how you feel about that too," she continued, "but it wasn't Ted's fault. I don't even blame Johnny. It was sin that caused him to do what he did – his love of sin."

"Mother!" There was horror in her voice. "How can you talk that way? He killed Fritz! He got so drunk he didn't know what he was doing and drove his car right into Fritz. And you say it wasn't his fault? Fritz would still be alive if it hadn't been for him! Don't you know that?"

Mrs. McCloud did not answer. Nor did she tell her daughter that she had to fight the same bitterness, the same blind rage and desire for revenge. There would be time enough later to make that confession. She was afraid that if it was made at this moment, it would only fan Connie's resentment. She prayed silently for her daughter.

In a moment the girl continued. "I saw in the paper last night that they've let that–that killer out on bail."

"Yes," her mother said. "The reporter called the morning after the funeral and told us about it."

Anger twisted Connie's attractive features until she was almost ugly. "I wish they'd leave him in jail!"

* * *

That night Ted Larson came over to see Connie, a box of candy in his hand.

"Mr. McCloud, is–is Connie here?" His voice revealed something of the strain he was under.

"I'll call her. Won't you sit down?"

At first, she refused to come out of her bedroom. "I–I just don't want to talk to anybody," she said.

"Please come out, Connie," her dad urged, "even if you can only stay a minute."

"Who is it?"

Her dad did not answer her question directly. "You shouldn't keep a guest waiting."

She glanced in the mirror, patting her hair hurriedly into place, and followed her dad into the living room. When she saw Ted Larson, she stopped suddenly; the color drained from her cheeks leaving them a sickly yellow. Anger sparked in her eyes.

Ted got nervously to his feet. "Hello, Connie." She did not answer him.

"I–I know there's nothing I can say or do that–that will help any, but I–I want you to know how sorry I am for–for what happened."

She drew herself erect. "You should be sorry!" She rasped out the words. "You should be! Your drunken brother was driving the car that killed Fritz! Or doesn't that mean anything to you?"

Ted flinched as though she had slapped him in the face.

Mr. McCloud went over to where his daughter

was standing. "Connie!" he broke in sternly. "Please don't talk that way. It wasn't Ted's fault!"

Tears filled her eyes. "It wasn't Fritz' fault either!" she exclaimed, her voice trembling on the edge of hysteria. "But he's dead! Don't you know that, Daddy? *He's dead!*"

With that she turned and fled from the room. Her bedroom door slammed behind her.

For a minute no one in the room said anything. Ted Larson shifted uneasily from one foot to the other. Then Lester McCloud went over to him.

"I'm sorry Connie spoke the way she did, Ted," he said. "She's terribly upset right now. She'll feel differently after she's had time to think about it."

"I guess I had it coming," Ted said, more to himself than to Mr. McCloud. "You don't know how terrible we feel about this. I don't think any of us have slept since–since the accident."

Tears came to Vivian McCloud's eyes. "Tell your parents and–and Johnny that–that we don't blame anyone for the accident."

Ted choked. "I know Mom's going to be relieved to hear that you don't hold anything against us. She wanted to send some flowers, but she was afraid you wouldn't accept them."

When he got to the door to leave, he turned back momentarily. "I suppose I'd just as well leave this," he said, handing the candy to her, "I won't have any use for it."

Mrs. McCloud smiled compassionately. "Thank you, Ted. I'll give it to Connie in the morning."

"Th-thank you. I–I sure am glad I stopped by to talk to you tonight."

Lester McCloud spoke up quickly. "Would you take a message to Johnny for me?"

Ted started. "I–I suppose so."

"Tell him that we're praying for him."

Ted's eyes widened. He started to speak, but the words stuck in his throat. Tears coursed down his cheeks as he took Mr. McCloud's hand and shook it expressively.

When he was gone Mrs. McCloud moved closer to her husband and slipped her arm about his waist. Together they turned and went back to the sofa.

"The poor boy."

"I don't think I've ever seen anyone so miserable," Lester said. They sat down and for a time drew comfort from the nearness of each other. "Think how Johnny must feel. He and Fritz were friends."

"I was thinking about that." She was silent for a time. "You know, I'd like to go over to the Larson home next week and talk to his mother."

There was a short silence.

"That won't be easy. Do you think you can?"

"I can't go in my own strength, I know. When I allow myself to think about what's happened, I get to feeling the same as Connie does. But with God's help I can go over and talk to her."

* * *

Ted Larson had only been gone a short while when there was another knock on the door. When Lester McCloud answered it, he was surprised to see the visitor on the porch.

"W-won't you come in?"

"I–I–" Sweat pearled the boy's sallow face and his gaze met Mr. McCloud's briefly. Then it lowered as though he couldn't stand to look into the older man's eyes. He swallowed forcibly.

"I–I–I'm Johnny Larson!"

There! It was out! He waited, expecting Mr. McCloud to fly into a rage. Instead, hurt gleamed momentarily in his eyes and he had difficulty speaking, but that was all.

"Come in, Johnny." His voice was quiet and kindly. I've been wanting to talk to you."

Numbly the boy came into the living room and allowed himself to be ushered to a chair. Fritz' dad sat down beside him. Finally, Johnny looked up.

"I–I–I thought–." Tears came to his eyes. "I had to come over and–and tell you how sorry I am, but I–I thought–." He could not continue.

"I'm glad you came, Johnny," Lester told him.

"I didn't mean to run into Fritz' car and kill him. I want you to know that!"

Lester McCloud nodded. "I know you didn't do it purposely, Johnny. But everything goes wrong when sin is controlling our lives." He explained to the distraught boy how sin was the cause of all his problems, including his drinking. But Jesus Christ loved him and had given His life so that he might be saved from sin and its penalties.

"Fritz used to talk to me about those same things," Johnny said, his lips curling bitterly. "If I'd only listened, everything would be different. But I didn't! Jesus wouldn't save me now, not after what I've done."

"That's where you're wrong," Mr. McCloud continued quietly. "God doesn't recognize any degrees of sin, Johnny. Christ died to save you as surely as He died to save Fritz. He's longing to forgive you."

Tears began coursing down Johnny's cheeks as Mr. McCloud continued to talk to him about the Lord. At last Johnny dropped to his knees to accept Christ as his Savior. Lester McCloud knelt beside him. As he did so an overwhelming sense of joy and peace surged over him. Fritz had sown the seed, but God had given him the privilege of reaping the harvest.

Truly God was shaking Fairview with the accident that resulted in Fritz' death.

THE
DANNY ORLIS
SERIES

The Danny Orlis series, by Bernard Palmer, delivers a blend of adventure, mystery, and suspense through various settings—from the Canadian wilderness to Guatemalan jungles. Danny Orlis, an adept outdoorsman, skilled athlete, and committed Christian, employs his quick thinking, calm bravery, and biblical solutions to confront everyday problems and hair-raising dangers. Early stories focus on Danny navigating school life, sports, and outdoor challenges, while in later books, Danny and his wife Kay provide wisdom and guidance to youngsters facing lifelike situations and challenges. Having sold over two million copies, this series has made Palmer a renowned author in Christian youth literature. Palmer is also the author of the Felicia Cartright series and various other series for Christian youth.

AVAILABLE FROM WWW.ANEKOPRESS.COM

www.ingramcontent.com/pod-product-compliance
Lightning Source LLC
Chambersburg PA
CBHW060501300726

48975CB00008B/2592